ANGEL'S
DEVIL
A JAKE BRAND, PI, STORY

M. LOUIS

Editing by Kristin Thiel
Book design by Vinnie Kinsella
Printed in the United States of America
ISBN: 978-0-9863196-0-0

To Linda, my devilish angel

Contents

Monday, July 11

2:00 p.m.
"Would you like a bloody thumbprint..." Jake

The scorching sun shows no pity to a hump like me, laid out in the open on the high desert terrain. Bugs try to seek shelter in my clothing, but they crawl along my bare skin until they become trapped within a fold of fabric or drown in a drop of my sweat. The dryness of the air would shrivel me like a discarded orange peel but for the large quantity of water that I consume. Just an average day on recon. First, I surreptitiously move to a location with a clear view of my target's haunt. Then, I wait long days that progress hour upon monotonous hour. I try to avoid all movement while constantly searching for my prey. I remain hidden under natural and man-made camouflage for days, hoping for a brief window of opportunity to open. And when it does, I shoot. My weapon might be a sniper rifle with high-velocity bullets or a camera with heat-sensitive imaging and facial-recognition capabilities, or it might be a laser that provides a target for a smart bomb. Whatever the mission, it always comes down to the brief moment when I focus my vision on a precise image and gently squeeze a trigger...The image fades and reforms as a conference room.

As much as I hated those times in the wild, they were a cake walk compared to this. Sitting in a twentieth-floor conference room with a view of East Portland, and snow-clad Mount Hood piercing a deep-blue, cloudless sky, I press my palms against the long table made from a single slab of old-growth fir. Its gnarled grain and occasional knots provide a welcome diversion from the conversation circling me like a hungry vulture. My chair is more comfortable than my bed—that's a blessing. And the room is stocked with coffee, water, tea, and soft drinks. Nobody would want me to not be able to dig my own grave because of a dry throat. But if they really wanted me to spill the beans, they'd have some whiskey on hand. To my right sits Peter Jennings, my attorney. Directly across from me sits my wife, Sue Brand. Next to her sits her attorney, the evil stepmom from every Disney movie, Sally Crenshaw, or Sal, as she is apt to remind me.

The two attorneys are charging ten bucks a word, triple for words with four or more syllables, and must be keeping score as they compete for the title of Most Verbose. I glance at my wife, the love of my life. Her short brown hair frames her normally smiling face. Today that face is tense, uncertain. She can't, or won't, return my gaze; I think she's ready for us to finally end. What happened? How could the overwhelming passion and need for each other when we married have turned into her overwhelming need to run? She says I've changed, that I'm more serious with bouts of melancholy mixed in. I'm sure I have changed—isn't that part of life? How could I not? She's changed as well. But a marriage is forever, and change is going to happen. Shouldn't we be working through this? Not according to her mom. Sue's mom says marriage is forever or until her little baby is unhappy, whichever occurs first.

"Jake? Are you going to answer the question?" Sue asks.

I break free of my thoughts and focus on the room. "What question?" I ask. I feel everyone staring at me, trying to decipher the nature of my mental disability.

"Do you affirm that all assets have been accurately listed on the inventory sitting in front of you?" Attila the Sal asks.

I look at Pete, who nods toward the sheet of paper sitting in front of me. All of our worldly possessions are individually listed. Each item is assigned to the person who will take full ownership in a few moments. This treasure chest of riches is to be split four ways, one share to Sue, one to me, and one to each of our attorneys.

"Yes, it looks correct. Oh, wait a sec, Pete, it doesn't show the bottle return deposits. I'll bet I have twenty bucks' worth, easy." I smile at the Sal-inater, trying my damnedest to annoy her. But she just smiles back at me while she twirls her black designer readers. Does this woman ever get angry? I've tried awfully hard to rile her and am saddened by my lack of success.

"Please sign where indicated," Sal-cula orders.

I look at her and imagine the crosshairs of my scope on her forehead. I narrow an eye to focus my aim. She winks at me, causing me to freeze as if my imaginary gun is pointed at me instead of her. Inside my brain, my little devil screams, "Pull the trigger!" Nearly simultaneously, my little angel urges me to ask her out. Out of the corner of my open eye, I see Sue frowning and shifting her gaze between me and her attorney. She sees the odd looks we're giving each other. I break free of my daydream, pick up a pen, and quickly scribble my name somewhat across the line provided.

"What now? Would you like a bloody thumbprint?" I ask the room. Nobody laughs but my little devil and Godz-Sal-A.

The attorneys begin to gather documents and stuff them into file folders and briefcases.

"Pete, it was good working with you on this. Here's your set of the signed documents; I'll have everything recorded today. Sue and Jake, you are officially single," Son of Sal says.

I look at Sue and see the tear that I feel. I want to hug her and promise her it was all a bad dream—we'll be okay. I want to promise that I'll change back to the man she loved. We can still be we. I want to smell the freshness of her hair, the sweet aroma of her perfume. I want to feel her body perfectly contoured to mine. But I don't even get a handshake. Sue stands, walks out of the conference room, and heads to the elevators, leaving Pete, Sal-itosis, and me to shake hands and bid adieu like civilized humans who have successfully completed the normal, everyday task of dismantling husband and wife.

When I shake hands with Sal the butcher, she squeezes a bit tighter than I expect, causing me to focus on her face, a surprisingly pretty face. An assertive "used to getting what it wants or destroying somebody" face. She mouths the words, *Call me.* Before I can turn and run, she turns and waves to Pete. I stand anchored to the floor, until Pete grabs my arm and pulls me toward the elevator.

"Drink?" I ask.

"Seems kind of early for that, don't you think?" Pete asks.

I give Pete my best "you ain't my mom" look. "I don't end my marriage very often, Pete. Are you in or are you out?"

He nods and says, "You're right. It's been a tough day. Sure, one drink isn't the end of the world."

5:00 p.m.
"Not as quick as Ninja Sal..." Jake

The East Bank Saloon is a great place to grab a burger and a beer. Its rustic interior matches the nearly 120-year-old facade. Pete goes inside to find a table and order a round while I stand on the sidewalk, the required ten feet from the entrance to the restaurant, taking a long, hard drag on a cigarette. Being banned from smoking inside a bar in the great state of Oregon makes me feel like a leper. The pedestrians who purposely swerve around my haze of spent smoke confirm my feeling with their grimaces. I perfected the smoking habit in the army. Spending long days and nights on base with nothing to do, I found a smoke could calm my nerves. But the habit began when I was a kid. I remember my dad and his buddies smoking like wood-powered locomotives, guzzling cases of Olympia beer, and playing pinochle. I loved to sit and watch, until they finally let me start playing at fourteen, and drinking at fifteen.

"Those are going to kill you," Pete says when I finally make my way to my chair.

"Not as quick as Ninja Sal."

"Ninja, you say? I was getting the vibe that maybe you two were into each other. I saw you winking at her."

"You got it all wrong, Pete, ol' pal—that wasn't a wink. I was focusing my Leupold & Stevens scope on the bridge of her nose. I didn't want to miss," I say.

"No reason to hide your carnal desire, Jake—you're a free man. You can start looking for the next ex–Mrs. Brand."

"Damn, Pete, that's awfully dark. Is that what you think about marriage? It's just the beginning of the divorce?"

"Not for everyone, Jake, but for you? If you want to be happily married, you need to find your best friend. I didn't see that between you and Sue. Until you find that person, you won't stick."

I look at Pete's face. He looks way younger than he is. His eyes are caring, but his mouth is intense. He's not joking with me; he's trying to educate me. "I think I liked it more when you were lecturing me on smoking."

"I'm not lecturing, Jake; I'm observing. You're a good man. I can see it; Sue could see it; that's why she waited as long as she did before she couldn't take it any longer. Hell, even Sally can see it. But you have a layer of armor surrounding your heart, and a loose wire in your brain. You have to risk being hurt to build relationships. Were you always this closed off? Maybe something about the army..."

Something about the army. That's what all well-intentioned folks who've never been in the military say. I think back to before the army and remember the pain of losing the first love of my life. "It was life before the army that closed me off, not the other way around." I pause to remember. "Everyday life is at least as dangerous as anything I experienced in the military. There you generally know who the enemy is, what they want to do, and why they want to do it. In real life everyone acts like they're your friend, but half of them are trying to get into your wallet. I can't figure out who falls into which half. That part of my brain isn't working well yet. So, to me trust equals danger."

"So, you don't like risk, and you don't trust people? You have a dark mark on your soul, Jake Brand."

He smiles as he says it, but it sounds sad to me. Am I a lost cause, and everyone knows it but me?

"Jake, unlike you, I have to head home. I have a wife who has expectations, and I intend to meet them. At least tonight I'm going to meet them. Give you a lift?"

"I'm good to drive myself."

"You going to make poker this week?"

"Yeah, I'll be there. Later, buddy." I watch as the happily married man leaves. His presence is required at home, and he is thankful for it.

"Waitress, could I have another beer? Thanks."

Tuesday, July 12

11:00 a.m.
"But the cocktails aren't helping..." Sarah

As I walk into my office, I'm greeted with, "You're late," by my assistant, Sarah Genton. Sarah used to work for the LAPD but quit because her fiancé moved to Portland. She's been with me for approximately a year and has slowly improved our technology skill sets. Sarah also has become one of my best friends. She's attractive, smart, and most important, doesn't take any crap from me.

"No, I'm not—I'm early."

Sarah's intense blue eyes lock onto me like lasers just before a smart bomb explodes. She squares her shoulders to me and places her fists on her hips. I can tell she isn't getting my humor. "Jake, you were supposed to be here at nine to meet with Jack French. Remember? We were to go through our findings?"

Jack is an attorney whose client is being criminally prosecuted for theft. His client, Bob Sexton, is an accountant for a small trucking firm. Recently the owner discovered that somewhere in the neighborhood of $250,000 has disappeared from the firm's coffers over the past three years. Bob's been the accountant the entire time. Based upon his ability to access the money, a spicy new car, and a deposition from the wife of the owner of the trucking firm, Bob is the chief suspect. Jack hired us to see if we could support Bob's strenuous objection to the accusation.

"Oh, I forgot. Did you reschedule?"

"No, I met with him and went through our findings."

"What did he say?"

"At first he was pissed that you weren't here. I thought he might fire us. But I went over the materials with him, and he left a happy camper."

The materials include a documented trail of money from the firm's accounts to the owner's wife's accounts. It seems she decided to blame Bob for her withdrawals. She set up an account in Bob's name at a local bank. Since she worked for the firm, she had access to all of his identification. It happens that she has a boyfriend who bears a close enough similarity to Bob that he can pass for Bob. The wife would wire funds from the firm's account to the fake Bob's account. Fake Bob would go to the bank and pull cash out. Turns out fake Bob writes left-handed on the bank security footage, whereas the real Bob is right-handed.

"Good. I mean, not good that I missed the meeting. Good he was happy. I can't believe the cops couldn't figure this out."

"Budget cuts, according to Jack. Jake, it was uncomfortable. You can't not deliver on promises to clients and leave me caught in the middle."

I nod and say, "You're right. I'll be more aware of my calendar in the future."

Sarah softens her stance and looks at me with concern. "Anyway, how did it go yesterday?"

"I'm single."

"It's going to work out, Jake, just give it some time. But the cocktails aren't helping. You're drinking too much. I saw it in LA. Cops have a bad couple of weeks and think they can run and hide in an alcoholic haze. You need to slow down. Hell, take some time off. Alvera and I can handle the office."

“Thanks, Sarah, but I’ll be fine.”

“Sure, eventually.” She looks at me, and I read doubt across her face. “Okay, you’re a big boy. I’m going to head out and do some interviews on the Alberty case. What’s your schedule?”

“I have a rendezvous with the wayward Mr. Cheevers and his mistress tonight. Get some pics to finish the case.”

“Good, be careful. I’ll have my cell on if you run into any problems.”

“Thanks, call me if anything pops in the interviews.”

10:55 p.m.
“Their whispers are sweet and low...” Jake

The street is dark but for light emitting from behind window blinds of the paramours’ home. The air is warm and comfortable as I sit in my Jeep and smoke. Mr. Cheevers has been in the house with Jenny Not-Mrs.-Cheevers for about an hour, and it’s about time for me to get into position. Mrs. Cheevers is convinced Mr. Cheevers is cheating. Turns out she has good instincts. This is the third night in the past two weeks that I’ve managed to catch the cheating Cheevers here. So far I haven’t had any luck obtaining pictures to prove he’s the cheater I know he is, and my patience is wearing thin. I take a final drag on the cigarette and toss it through the open window, watch the red glow arc out and down, explode and scatter in different directions upon impact with the asphalt. I grab my camera and step out into the sultry July evening. I haven’t seen any pedestrians in the ninety-plus minutes I've been waiting. I've already scouted out where I'm going. Earlier this week I came dressed as a utility worker and walked the yard when no one was home. There weren't any security measures I could find. No dog, no motion detectors, no claymore mines.

In back of the house is a children's swing play set. It's one of those puzzles that the big box stores sell to do-it-yourselfers. From behind it, I have a clear view of the master bedroom, which has graciously been walled with glass. The windows are open, trying to catch a breeze. The sheer curtains move occasionally but for the most part hang motionless. I can see the shadows of two people dancing behind them, but I can't get a clean picture because the breeze is too light to move the sheers. My camera is equipped with a directional mic, which is wired to my ear. Through it, I can hear the soft, melodic sounds of Al Green: "Don't you know that I'm still in love, in love with you."

The dancers disappear, and the lights dim a bit. I look through my camera, which magnifies everything greatly, but still can't find an angle to get a clean picture. I decide that if I want to get pictures I'll have to take some risk. I have to move closer, slowly and as quietly as I can. I navigate the yard, careful not to trip on a rake or skateboard. There's more light inside the room than outside, so it's unlikely that the couple can see through the curtains at the moment. Still, to be safe, I try to camouflage my silhouette as much as I can by keeping bushes in front of me along the inhabitants' line of sight. I reach the windows and carefully extend the camera lens between the sheers and into the room, but just barely, just an inch or so past the edge of the curtains. I can see shapes in bed with my bare eyes. With the enhanced images of the camera, I can see them as if they were in broad daylight. Their whispers are sweet and low, their bodies move in rhythm to the music. I hear her moan as he whispers, "Oh, baby." I set the camera to movie mode and begin to record their intimacy. I feel my own heat grow as I watch in secret. I should feel bad about trespassing on their passion, but I don't. I feel I'm part of their moment. I don't see Cheevers and Jenny; I see Sue and me. I see what we had and lost.

Suddenly they stop moving, and Cheevers looks toward the window. "Did you hear something, baby?"

I freeze as my little devil asks, "You can't even sneak up on a couple of people that are grabbing at each other? When did you become such a clodhopper?"

I'm about to backhand my little devil when Not-Mrs.-Cheevers says, "There's nothing there—it's just the music. Come here, don't stop, not now."

He hesitates, his animal instinct telling him to check out the noise. But his lust wins out. "Sure, baby. Sure."

Once they've regained their pace, I slowly retreat, moving back around the house to my car, all by myself.

Wednesday, July 13

7:00 p.m.
"A beast that drags me into the darkness..." Jake

Sitting in the Driftwood Room and drinking alone is probably a poor decision. The soft, tan leather seating, dark paneling, and Sammy Davis Jr. song give it the feel of the '60s. For a short time, I can avoid the world and try to forget the past. Tonight it's quiet: just a bartender, a couple in love, and me. On a Timbers soccer game night, the place fills with scarf-waving hooligans, but that's not tonight. I watch the couple and decide that they are newly infatuated. He smiles as she scratches her nose. She laughs when he tells a stupid joke. By now I know what to look for, and the signs of doom are there. There's nothing casual in their appearance or actions. Like Pete said, they don't seem to be best friends. No, I think the second hand has begun its inescapable countdown to their arrival in Splitsville—while I sit by myself with an empty hourglass. No more sand for Sue and me. I'm single with time on my hands and no one to spend it with.

I can't help but think about the good times with Sue. Our honeymoon in Hawaii was amazing. We spent two weeks in the sun and bed, sun and bed, bed and bed; I do remember one dinner. Her tanned body was beautiful, especially her tan lines. I close my eyes, but already the depth of the memories is fading. No more Sue, now I get to find a new miss—lucky me. I debate between going outside for a smoke and ordering another drink. Whiskey wins. Before my drink arrives, my phone buzzes.

"Jake Brand."

"Mr. Brand, sorry to disturb you. This is Sal Crenshaw."

"Ah yes. Well, I'm sorry, but I've already donated blood today. You'll have to wait six weeks."

"Ha-ha, no blood this time, just your signature. I have another paper I need you to sign. Pete has already approved it and said I should go straight to you. Unfortunately, your divorce isn't official until I get the signature, and Sue really wants to move forward. Could I meet you somewhere?"

Based upon the number of words the Sal-manian Devil has used, this phone call has already cost Sue about $500. "Sure, you know where the Driftwood Room is?"

"Yes, the Hotel DeLuxe, near the ballpark. I'll be there in less than fifteen minutes."

"See you then." The line goes dead, and I put my phone away. The emotion of the past few weeks spent huddling with Pete and clashing with Sal and Sue rises back to the surface. I thought I was starting to beat it down. But no, it's just below the first layer of skin cells, waiting for the slightest scratch or change in wind current to free it to the surface. There it crawls about and eventually grows into a beast that drags me into the darkness of failure. I down my drink and order another.

True to her word, Sal arrives in less than fifteen minutes. She sits. "What are you drinking?"

"Why? Do you charge differently based upon the alcohol being consumed?"

She smiles. "No, I think I'll join you. Barkeep? One for me, and it looks like my gentleman friend could use another."

"Not that I don't appreciate your greasing my hangover but *gentleman friend*? Not what I expected to hear."

"Oh, you're a gentleman, I can see that. And I hope we

can be friends. I know I can be tough on people, but I have to zealously represent the interests of my client."

"I suppose, but do you have to enjoy it so much? I mean, you're crazy mean."

She laughs loudly as the drinks arrive. "Thank you, Jake, that's quite a compliment. Cheers." She finishes her drink in a single motion and signals for another round. Not to be beat by her yet again, I follow suit.

"What's next for you, Jake? Do you already have the next Mrs. Brand picked out?"

"I hope your tongue bursts into flames. No way is there going to be another Mrs. Brand. I'm swearing off women until all attorneys are dead."

"That seems like an overreaction. Plus, I've heard it before. Men always seem to think they have control over their emotions and sexuality. But within a month, you all cave and find passion, infatuation, and then love. I give you six weeks tops."

"What about women? How long do they hold out?"

"They don't. Women want a man to listen to them, provide a sense of security and belonging. Women are looking right away but fearful they'll never find Mr. Right because he's already taken."

"What about you? Are you anchored in some guy's harbor?"

"Not at the moment. I'm not like most women. I'm not looking for a life partner, not yet anyway. But I do love men. Not one man, mind you—men, plural. Another drink?"

"Sure." Only to me it sounds like, "Slurrr." I can tell that the alcohol has just invalidated my driver's license. It's another cab for me. We chat about our pasts without really listening. My little devil hears, "Blah, blah, blah." We finish the latest around, and we both show signs of being ready to leave; she stands up with her purse, and I contemplate the bottom of my glass.

"So, Jake, it's been fun, but I should probably get going. How are you getting home? You don't seem very capable of driving at the moment."

"You couldn't be more right, Ms. Sal. I'm going to hail a cab and ride in luxury."

"No need for a cab—I can give you a lift. Where do you live?"

I begin to refuse her offer, but as I stand, the room sways a bit. I decide that waiting for a cab would be inconvenient. I give her my address, and she pays the bill: nice, a chauffeur who picks up the bar tab.

Thursday, July 14

7:00 a.m.
"Iceberg dead ahead..." Jake's little devil

The sunlight burns my retinas through my closed eyelids. I cover my head with my pillow to save my sight and roll onto my side just as the blankets and sheets are thrown off of me.

A hard, full-handed smack on my buttocks bounces me into the air. "What the hell?"

"Up, Power Ranger—I made coffee and toast. I couldn't find any eggs. Plus, I still need your signature."

My eyes see a shape moving about. I have a creepy sense that I recognize the voice from some horror movie. I try to place it, but all I get are images of mass murderers. I begin to check off my list of sinister characters until I get to Attila the Sal. Holy mother of God, what is she doing here? More important, why is she spanking my bare ass? My eyes focus just in time to see her shed my bathrobe and then dress, with her back to me. "You are one sick bastard, Jake Brand," says my little angel. "What a ride, though. That dame is an animal," says my little devil. "No, no, no, no, not true," I say.

"What's that? Did you say something?" fire-breathing Sal asks.

"I said okay. Get up, coffee, toast, paper—all good." I rise up onto my elbows and rub my eyes. I look around and find I have my room to myself. I sit up fully too quickly, and the room spins a bit. I wait a moment to grab my robe. I knot the bathrobe tie as tightly as I can to prevent a redo of what I can't remember. I walk into the kitchen and sit at the table in front of a steaming mug of coffee, a plate of toast, and some of my mother's homemade jam. Wouldn't mom be proud?

"I need your signature here. Do you have a pen nearby?"

"Yeah, drawer." I point.

"Here, good. Okay. Jake, what a lovely evening; we'll need to do this again. I'll give you a call."

"Did she just give you the 'don't call me, I'll call you' line?" my little angel asks.

I'm a sick, sick man. I'm certain I'd feel humiliated and cheap if I could remember what happened. How did I get here? I mean, besides the fact that I live here. Oh yeah, whiskey.

"Well, Jake, I hate to, you know, bada-bing and run. But I need to get home and clean up. I have stuff to do. Why don't you throw some clothes on, and I'll give you a ride to your car."

Every time she says something, I feel her chomping off pieces of my flesh. "Sure, I'll be back in a jiff," I say.

As I enter the bedroom, I see just how active we were. The bed coverings are all over the place. An ashtray has spilled onto the carpet; empty beer bottles lie on the dresser table. Oh my, this image is going to leave a mark. As I dress, I call to her, "Why the hurry to get my signature?"

"It's that Jason character—can't get you two apart fast enough."

Jason? Who's Jason? "Iceberg dead ahead," my little devil says. I walk back out into the living room wearing pants, no shirt, and a "what the hell?" look on my face. I see Sal looking at the floor and shaking her head. She looks up at me and reads me like a shark reads the splashes of a seal.

"You don't know, do you?" she asks.

"Obviously not, but I can bet I'm about to."

"Sue...well, she has been seeing someone. After you moved out, she found a friend who lent a shoulder, which became a comforting hug, which became—"

"Jesus, enough." I turn my palm toward her to stop the shrill truth from biting through me. I sit down on my couch and rub my face. I can't get my mind wrapped around the fact that Sue moved on before we were split. Oh my, oh my. This is by far the worst day of my life. I thought the day at the law offices signing documents was tough. This is tough times excruciating.

"Don't get your undies in a twist, Jake. It was going to happen. Hell, just think about how much pain you won't have to suffer through in the future."

"Swell, Sal, that's just peachy keen."

Her laugh sounds truly amused and grates like sandpaper on my brain.

"Hey, I have an answer for you."

I look at her, confused yet again. "What was the question?"

"Which nickname I like the most, silly. The list of she-devil nicknames you ticked off for me last night? I like Sal-inator and Attila the Sal the best. Okay, okay, the clear winner is Attila the Sal. You can call me Tilly for short."

How is it possible that just when I think I'm scraping the cement floor of my soul, this creature is able to use me as a pile driver to create a crevasse? "How sweet."

"I thought so. Go ahead, call me Tillie—I want to hear it roll off your tongue." Her smile is taunting.

"Time to leave, Sally."

"Sure, come on, let's go."

"No, you go. I think I need some quiet time."

11:30 a.m.
"You're hungover every day..." Sarah

Sarah and I meet for lunch to go over our current case files. We have two. I'm having problems reading the pages with my sunglasses on. But to take the sunglasses off is to expose my sensitive eyes to the glaring light.

"You're scheduled to meet with Mrs. Cheevers today to review the footage and talk about the next step. Do you want me there?" asks Sarah.

"No, I can handle it. I don't think she'll be particularly surprised."

"Here's our final billing. Make sure to get a check."

"Roger."

"Next is the Sexton case. French passed our info to the prosecutor, who is going to drop the charges against Bob. But he's also asked that Bob be wired and attempt to get the wife to incriminate herself. French has asked that we be involved with the police just to make sure that Bob isn't being tricked or entrapped."

"If the police will let us, it's fine with me. You okay handling?"

"Sure, the police have already signed off on it, with some conditions." She hands me a sheet of paper, and I read through the conditions requested by the police.

"I'd add one of our own. If at any point we see legal or physical risk to our client, we end the process, no questions asked."

"I'll let them know. If they balk, I'll tell them Bob isn't interested."

"Perfect. Anything else?"

"No, that's all we need to catch up on at the moment."

I watch as she gathers her notes, neatly aligns the pages, and places them in folders. She's been amazing to have around. She's been managing the day-to-day office tasks as well as me. I feel more relaxed, and clients seem happier. She brushes a wisp of hair off of her face, looks up at me, and smiles. "What?" she asks.

"Nothing, I'm just, well. Sarah, you've been here long enough that I think it's time for a personnel review."

Her eyes become brighter with unpleasant intensity. "Is there a problem?"

"No, you're doing great. I just wanted you to know that I'm really happy you're here."

A smile returns to her face and warms me like the rising sun. "I'm glad, Jake. I really like it here."

"Good."

"But there is one thing," she says.

"Oh boy, not a raise already?"

"No, not money—at least not yet. No, I'm still concerned about you. You're dragging, and I know you're hung over. Listen to me, stop drinking, and take better care of yourself."

I look at her for a second and then look away as I think about a response. "I can handle it. I'm just going through a tough period."

"I know you are, and I have empathy for you. But you aren't handling it well. And I'm not the only one who's noticed. Both Pete and Carl have asked about you recently. We're all concerned."

She looks at me, ginning up the courage to insert the serrated edge of the truth deeper. She takes a deep breath and pushes. "When you hired me, you said this job is dangerous. I agree with you—it can be. We both need to know we can rely on each other in a pinch. Right now, I don't know if I can rely on you. You're hungover every day, you miss meetings, and often you seem to be lost in a daydream. I think your drinking is negatively affecting your work."

My face stings; I want to tell her she's wrong, that I can handle my own affairs, thank you very much. But I hesitate. I feel hurt and angry. I look into Sarah's eyes, and I don't see pleasure or judgment; I just see sincerity and concern. She's not doing this for fun—she feels she has to. I can tell that was tough for her to say. It would be tough for anyone. If I'm a bastard, I'll jump on her. If I'm a drunk, I'll brush her off.

I nod my head. "Message received. Thanks."

"You sure? We're good?"

I smile. "Better than good. Let's get to work."

5:00 p.m.
"I'm shocked into silence..." Jake

Sitting in my office all alone, I contemplate the message Sarah delivered. My drinking is impacting my job performance. "Hey, man, it's not like you're drinking on the job," my little devil says. I think about my failed marriage and the frustration I've created for Sarah. If I'm being honest with myself, I'm angry. I don't know why I'm angry, but I am. I light a cigarette, blow smoke rings toward the open window, and watch as they dissipate just before they can escape the confines of the office. I've seen guys who've lost themselves in the bottle. It isn't pretty, and they're always the last to know. But I also know I'm not drinking nearly as much as I did when I was in college. Sarah's wrong—the problem isn't booze; it's my messed-up personal life. I need to refocus and start moving on.

I hear the outer office door open and close. Alvera's gone for the day, so I have to be my own receptionist. I look toward my doorway, but the door is mostly closed, so I can't see who just entered the outer office. I stand. "Hello? May I help you?" I reach the door and open it and come face-to-face with my longest-running dream.

"Hello, Jake."

My whole body tenses. I hear this voice at night sometimes, saying my name. Standing in front of me is the first love of my life, Heather Petermen. We haven't spoken in years. Not since I married Sue, if memory serves me. In my mind, she's still the beautiful, happy kid we all used to be. In front of me, for real, her blue eyes are sadder, her silky brown hair shorter. But she's stunning nonetheless, dressed in casual slacks and a frilly pink blouse.

"Heather, my God, what a surprise. I...I'm shocked." I move toward her with my arms wide to embrace her.

She quickly moves forward and tightly wraps her arms around me. I sense that this isn't a "gosh, it's great to see you" hug. This is an "I'm in trouble" grasp for help. The slight puffiness around her eyes tells me she's been crying.

"I know, it's been so long." She steps back and examines me. "You look different, Jake. I can't put my finger on it. But you look terrific."

"You haven't changed. Come in; have a seat."

"Thanks. I'm sure you're wondering why I'm here." She fidgets with her wedding ring.

"She's a mind reader," my little devil says. My little angel shushes him.

"I hadn't got to that yet—I'm still in shock. What has it been, six, seven years since we've seen each other?"

"Something like that. I've missed you, Jake. I've meant to contact you, but you know. Life just seems to get in the way." She looks down at her hands.

"What's up, Heather? What's on your mind?"

"Jake, I have bad news." She hesitates a moment and then looks at me. "Tony is dead."

I'm shocked into silence. Tony, Heather, and I were best friends as kids. We did everything together until Tony and Heather became a thing. Then I drifted away. Even though I haven't seen Tony in years, I feel sorrow creeping into my mind.

"It was a hit-and-run. The police didn't catch the driver; they're treating his death as a homicide. I don't know what to do. I'm..." She begins to cry, softly, tears of a woman who has been crying for a while. I walk around my table and embrace her. She weeps quietly on my shoulder. I hurt with each soft sob as I try to get my bearings. Tony's dead, and Heather is in my arms.

11:00 p.m.

"Change feels like my chauffeur to despair..." Jake

Heather told me what she knew, which wasn't much. I told her to give the police time to figure things out. And that I was happy to help any way I could. She told me she'd keep me informed and let me know the date and location of the funeral.

My mind is twisted like a pretzel, a badly formed, overly twisted pretzel. Tony's dead; Heather is back in my life, at least for a moment; Sue is off with Jason; and Sarah is concerned I'm drinking too much. I decide I need a drink. I remember Tillie and decide I need three. I find a new tavern, one with four walls, a ceiling, a long bar with stools, and a lot of alcohol containers displayed in front of a mirror. It's the Fill-in-the-Blank Tavern, but I'm invisible there, just another guy, not a regular. A few whiskeys will help me think through my collapsing universe. I know I need change, but change feels like my chauffeur to despair. And he's driving like a demon.

Sarah's right: I'm a danger on the job. My hands are shaky; I lack concentration, and most of the time I don't give a damn. Maybe this is part of what drove Sue away. No, she was gone long before I increased my drinking. As I think about Sue, I can't help but compare her with Heather. Sue and I never had magic like I did with Heather. Sue and I weren't soul mates; we were roommates. The more I think about Sue, the more I realize that she saved us a lot of pain by leaving me when she did. I was so concerned about being a failure that I lost sight of what was important. Pete's right: Sue was never my best friend.

I finish my drink, only my fourth. One more, I tell myself, and I'll head home and get a good night's sleep. "Bartender, another, please?"

"Last call, buddy. No more after this." He picks up a glass to begin to pour.

"Getting cut off in a dump like this?" asks my little devil. What the hell? Even strangers see what a wreck I've become. "Sure, but make it a double, asshole," I say.

The bartender turns back and looks at me, then sets the glass down. "Changed my mind. You're done. How about I call you a cab?"

"Fuck you, you pissant. You're not my mom. You offered another drink, and I want another drink. Then I'll get the hell out of here and tell the world what a prick you are. What's your name, by the way? I don't want to smear all the bartenders, just the dick." My little angel is pounding at the bars of the cage I've confined him in. My little devil says, "You don't need a lecture right now. You need to punch something."

"Mister, you need to leave before you get hurt. You're a drunk and need to get some counseling. But right now you need to vamoose."

"Oooh, fancy talk from a little jerk-off."

"Frank," he yells, "this guy needs to be gone."

I feel a paw the size of a grizzly's drop on my shoulder and practically push me to the floor. I grab the outside edge of the paw and twist it back against itself, causing Frank the bear to drop to his knees, screaming in pain.

"Now, Frank, you're old enough to know that little pricks like what's-his-face are only going to get you hurt." I twist Yogi's paw a bit more, and he screams again.

"You bastard, I'm going to kill you," Smokey growls.

"Whoa, Frank. You're not leaving me with many options. Let's see, release you and die is option one. Option two is I break your wrist and stomp your nose into your face. Hmmm, I'm thinking option one...no, number two. Yeah let's go with option two." I twist a bit harder just before the lights go out.

Friday, July 15

3:00 a.m.
"I wonder which one is going to lead the service..." Jake

I slowly become aware of movement and sound. But mostly I smell the end of the world. The stench that is eroding my nasal passages is a sweet combination of sweat, puke, and at least three other even worse odors I fear to identify. I open my eyes and see shoes, Converse high-tops, pointed at my face. Is this guy standing on the ceiling? No, I'm flat on a sticky floor. I look up and see a youthful face looking down at me.

"Hey, sleeping beauty; welcome to Shangri-la."

I look around and see benches of men in various stages of disarray. And to my chagrin, I see metal bars along one wall. Ah, I know this place. My little angel has escaped his cell and says, "You practically have a reserved seat here." I'm in the drunk tank. Why in the world am I in the drunk tank? Then memories of Winnie the Pooh and my final call seep into my brain. Oh yeah, that's why.

"What time is it?" I ask.

The youth looks past and then back to me. "About four in the morning."

I sit up at the same pace that I groan. I look around and spot a corner bench seat. I stand and groggily move to claim it. I sit and watch my fellow worshippers. Who would have thought there were this many of us on any given night? I wonder which one is going to lead the service. Where does the choir form? I guess we're all in the choir, moaning and snoring in an unorchestrated testament to stupidity.

I can't stop my brain from racing. I touch a lump on the back of my head and set off a whole new stinging ache. I feel horrible about the way I treated the bartender and Gentle Ben. Oh my God, did I break his wrist? If not, it was close. But it doesn't take long to refocus on Heather and Tony. Tony's dead, and Heather needs my help. Then there's Sue, who has moved on to greener pastures. And somehow scorched-earth Sal has moved into the void and filled me with more self-loathing. Self-pity to self-loathing to self-destruction—what can possibly be next? Oh, I know: self-damnation. My little devil chuckles.

At five in the morning a cop steps up to the bars. "Brand, Jake Brand. Where are you?"

"Here."

"It's your lucky day—time to go." He unlocks the cell door and waits for me to get up and exit. I stand and wobble through the gates of hell into the hallway of shame, which leads to freedom, I hope.

"Come on." He grabs my arm and guides me forward. He stops me at the door to an interrogation room. "Wait here." Oh crap, what now? I must have hurt Paddington Bear, and they're about to grill me.

From behind me I hear a familiar voice. "Hey, dumb shit, why are you standing there?" I turn and see Officer Milt Stanton, my one and only friend on the force. He and I worked a kidnapping case together a couple of years ago and saved a kid. Well, most of a kid—the kidnappers did remove a toe. Milt's in the process of retiring from the force and taking over the family business.

From atop his stubby frame, he shakes his head like he would at a child who just busted his mom's favorite flower pot.

"Like the look?" I ask.

"Funny, I like funny. 'Specially from a guy who came within a flea's whisker of being locked up for a couple of years for assault."

"Do fleas have whiskers?"

"You better hope they do, my friend. You better damn well pray they do. Do you remember what happened?"

We begin to walk in the direction of the exit, I hope. "I remember having a definitional issue with a gentleman at a bar—"

"Definitional?"

"Sure, he said one last drink. I said one last double, toe-may-toe, toe-mah-toe. You know, definitional."

"Right, what then."

"Well, I remember a grizzly named Frank on his knees and then...nothing. The world went black."

"I see. Let me fill in the blanks. Frank, the bouncer, was trying to remove you from the bar because you were being a jerk. You brought him to his knees and, according to Frank, threatened to break his wrist and stomp his nose in."

"I'm sure the way I said it, it sounded funnier. Did he mention he threatened to kill me?"

"No, but a couple of witnesses said they heard it. The world went dark when Jeffrey, the bartender, hit you over the head with a bat. You're lucky it was rubberized, otherwise you'd be dead. How does your cement noggin feel?"

"It feels terrible, just like every other part of my body."

"Good, you deserve to suffer. I saw your name flash on my computer, checked things out, and squared everything with Jeffrey and Frank."

"Squared it how?"

"I told them I thought you were acting in self-defense and that if they pressed charges, I'd have to bring them in as well. I also promised to have the next police function at the bar. Oh, and you have a lifetime ban. Don't want to forget that."

I nod in embarrassment. That crevasse in my soul just keeps getting deeper and deeper.

"Look, Jake, there have been three reports on you in the past six months. I can't help you after this. You have a problem, and it's spelled s-t-u-p-i-d. You're trying to kill yourself, which is a choice; just don't do it on my beat."

"You sound like you care," I say. "By the by, there's no reason to mention any of this to Sarah."

"Damn it, Jake, is that all you care about? Being outed to Sarah? How about caring about not being imprisoned for umpteen years?" Milt's face is flushed with anger. Here he is bailing a friend out, and all he's getting is grief. I think it's time to drag my ass out of the crevasse and begin climbing toward the light.

"Milt, I appreciate what you've done—I truly do. I'm sorry I'm being a jerk. It seems to be the only gear I have at the moment."

"You need treatment, Jake. I've done all I can. Your next stop is jail. Oh, wait, you've crossed that one off your list. I see guys like you too often. Some get it; most don't. Which are you?"

I feel shame for dragging my friend through my mess. "Thanks, Milt."

"You're welcome. Here's your cab. Go home, get some sleep, eat, and get some help. Got it?"

"I do." Crap. Last time I said that, it ended in divorce.

Wednesday, July 20

7:43 p.m.
"Time to thank my friends..." Jake

Carl's house is a fifteen-hundred-square-foot ranch in Cedar Hills, a bedroom community on the edge of Portland. It's comfortable and clean but is ready for a redo. He's hosting poker night, and I've just arrived with Sarah. We're the last ones. Carl is sitting at the poker table talking to Pete. Milt is standing nearby with an unlit cigar hanging from his mouth.

As we walk in, Carl gives Sarah a hug, and Milt gives me a light smack on the side of the head.

"Don't tell me you hold grudges," I say.

"Only when someone is suicidal," he replies.

I look around the room, and everyone seems to know what Milt's talking about.

"Quite the Chatty Cathy, aren't you," I say to Milt while shaking my head. "I'd hardly call an uncomfortable disagreement in a bar attempted suicide."

"That's not the way we see it," Carl says.

Carl is a former–Special Forces buddy of mine. He's rock hard and tough as nails. He hails from Texas, if you ask, though he's lived in Portland for the past three years. He usually avoids squabbles, preferring to be the strong silent type, but it looks like I've piqued his interest.

I decide it's time to change the subject. "Whose deal?" I ask. I may as well have said it to the wall. No one moves or says a word. I look at each of them, and they're all staring back at me. "What's up? Somebody die?"

"Jake," begins Pete, "we've been talking..."

"Who's we?" I calmly ask. I feel anger in my voice. Pete looks at me like I shouted at him.

His eyes become harder, more committed as he says, "All of us, we've all been talking, and we think you need to make some changes. You're ruining your health and risking your life and freedom, from what Milt's been sharing with us."

I look at Milt. "Et tu, Brute? Okay, let's get started. What kind of changes?" My face is hot, and my hands are clenched. I feel sweat forming on my upper lip and my heart racing. I know what's coming. I'm angry, not because they're confronting me, but because deep down I know they're right.

"Jake, you're killing yourself," Sarah says. "If you don't die of alcohol poisoning, you'll get it some other nasty way. Milt told us about the bartender. He could've killed you with that bat."

"But he didn't."

"But he could have. We know you're getting hammered most nights," Milt says. He looks at Sarah, who barely nods, confirming what everyone believes. "You're putting Sarah at risk. You're putting your entire life on the line because you're angry. And it's not just liquor. You're smoking too much. Hell, you were wheezing just walking out of the jail the other night. What are you angry about, Jake, losing Sue?"

Good question. Is this all about Sue? It's partly about Sue. Now I add Tony and Heather to the mix. What's my next step? I lose Sue, and I get drunk. I lose Tony and what, drugs? It seems that the angrier I become, the more that gets dumped on me. But there's more to it than just that. What am I railing at? "I didn't just lose Sue. I lost my identity. I lost the army and Sue, and as I'm sure you all know by now, my friend Tony. I have to start over again."

"I get that, Jake—I remember what you were like when you left the army. You grieved for it. You've grieved several bottles over. I lost the army too, Jake," says Carl. "And I miss it, I truly do, but life is about change. You either move on or you watch the blurred world from inside of a bottle. Is that what you want? You've seen that guy. Remember James?" I nod. "You know where he is now? Dead, drunk driving. And he left a wife and a kid to fend for themselves."

"Is she cute?" my little devil asks.

"I don't drive drunk," I say.

"Yet," says Pete. "But the way you're making decisions, it's just a matter of time."

I hang my head, my anger turning into embarrassment. When I was young, I believed that all I had to do was pray for help and forgiveness. All I had to do was put the burdens of my soul in God's hands and I could find peace and then happiness. Is that still an option? Will God listen? I look up at my friends and see love and concern etched in their faces. "I need a minute." I stand and leave the house. Outside, a warm breeze brushes against my skin. I hear the leaves of the trees rustle. I believe that God does speak to us every day. We just have to be open to the message, good or bad. Sometimes he comes to me through someone's smile, sometimes a beautiful sunset. "Oh my God, you're such a whiner," my little angel says. Sometimes he's pissed, and he puts the slowest driver in America in front of me. Tonight he's here, inside this house behind me. He's the voices of my friends, and I see the truth in what they're saying. I've known I was messing up for weeks, but I couldn't stop. No, that's not true. If I want to change, I have to be honest, at least with myself. I didn't want to stop. I wanted to escape. I turn and look back at the house. Inside is proof that I'm not a failure; I have friends who care about me. "Can we get back to punching out large furry creatures?" my little devil asks.

I glance back at the setting sun over the coast range. The dark crimson turning to orange trimmed in deep blue, as the sky darkens. It's time to change, time to thank my friends.

Sunday, July 24

3:15 p.m.
"Double or nothing, one field open..." Jake

"Thank you for gathering here to remember the life of Anthony Johnathan Weintraub, struck down in the prime of..."

The rustic church is small and full. At the altar the pastor is robed in black with a purple sash. He strikes a sad look as he reads the words that will close a chapter in my life. In front of him, the congregation sits quietly in the pews, dressed in somber colors. I find my attention drifting. I glance around at the symbols of my youth, when church was a cornerstone of my life. The depiction of the crucifixion behind the pastor. Angels floating on clouds carved into the railing of the balcony. And the stained-glass representations of Bible verses.

Burying a friend isn't something I ever anticipated. I guess that's pretty foolish. Unless you plan to be the first to go, this is inevitable. It's just that death was supposed to wait until we were older. Not that I haven't experienced death. I was in the army. And my father passed away not so long ago. But this feels like a detour onto a dark and foreboding road. It makes me anxious to think that I will travel it more frequently in the future.

Tony, Heather, and I went to the same schools, all the way through college. In grade school we were together constantly. In high school hormones were injected into our relationships, and things changed. In college we drifted apart.

Right after college, Tony and Heather married. I was happy for them but angry that it was Tony and not me she was marrying. I decided to strike out at them by enlisting in the army. That changed my life. Yet despite my best efforts, it had no visible impact on them.

"...ashes to ashes, dust to dust..."

In high school our favorite summer activity was to play double or nothing, one field open. The school field was a big dust bowl that was never watered. The game was a form of baseball that only required three players: a batter, pitcher, and outfielder. The batter would choose which field he wanted open, and the outfielder would move to play that field. The idea was for the batter to hit a pitch into the designated field on a fly. Then he had to run around first and on to second base. If he reached second before the outfielder could throw the ball to the pitcher, who had moved to cover second, the batter would score a run. If the batter hit a ground ball or hit the ball to the wrong field, if the outfielder caught the ball on the fly, or if the throw beat the runner to second base, he'd be out. Three outs and everybody switched positions.

One time I was at bat, Tony was pitching and Heather was in the outfield. I was tied with Tony—we each had eight runs—and Heather had seven. This was the last at bat. If I scored one more run, I won; if not, Tony and I tied. We really didn't like to tie.

"Hey, batter, batter! Hey, batter, batter!" yelled Tony as he threw a pitch. It was a terrible pitch aimed more at my head than the plate. But that didn't matter too much; there weren't any walks or strikeouts. Tony's strategy was to throw lots of wild pitches to frustrate me or tempt me into swinging at a bad one.

"You're so annoying, and a terrible pitcher. Oh, and I think I should remind you that you're ugly," I taunted him.

"You're just boring. Swing at a fucking pitch."

"Make a fucking pitch that's worth swinging at."

"All right, smart-ass, here it comes."

The next pitch was in the perfect spot over the plate. Tony threw it extra hard to make it tougher to hit. But he also knew that there was no way I could let this one go past. As soon as he threw the pitch, he turned and began to run for second base. I was completely focused on making contact with the ball. I could tell this was going to be the game winner. I turned and got my hips to flow through with the bat, and I smoked it. I followed the ball with my eyes as it jumped off the meaty part of my bat and scorched the air. Well, in my mind it scorched the air. It was a line drive and never rose to more than five feet off of the ground. I started running to first base. Before I made it two steps from the plate, I saw the ball hit Tony on the back of the head. He was lucky—it wasn't a square shot. The ball hit the curve near the top of his head and careened into center field. I sprinted around first as Tony hit the ground like a sack of potatoes. I could hear Heather screaming, asking Tony if he was okay. I didn't know if he was hurt or not. But I knew I could beat him to second base. I continued to sprint to second and touched it well before Heather ran past me without the ball.

I celebrated briefly, raising my hands to the excited crowd who cheered in my head. As the noise of the crowd died down, I decided maybe I should pretend to give a shit about Tony. I jogged over to him and kneeled on one side of him while Heather kneeled on the other. Tony's gray eyes were open, and he stared at the sky. He didn't say anything, but at least he was breathing.

"Is he dead?" Heather asked. Her eyes were serious, but her tone was light.

"I don't know—smell his pants," I replied.

"Smell his pants? I thought Tony was the one hit on the head, but you're the crazy one."

"Hey, it's a scientific fact that when you die your innards let go of all of your shit and pee. So, if you want to see if someone is dead, you smell their pants."

"*You* smell them. I'm not getting anywhere near poopy pants."

"Me neither. If he's dead who cares if his pants are crapped? Anyway, his eyes are moving. Hey, Tony, did you crap your pants?"

Slowly his eyes rolled like two gray marbles until he was staring at me. "You know you were out. I was in the infield when the ball hit me. It didn't get to the outfield on a fly," he said.

"Like hell. After it hit your granite block, it ricocheted into the outfield. Just ask Heather."

"Doesn't matter, it's in the rule book. If the ball hits a player in the infield, it's an infield hit, not an outfield hit."

"You dirty cheating son of a bitch. You know you lost. I'm about to get that ball and hit you with it again."

"Would you two stop cussing and fighting? You're both so ignorant," Heather said.

"*Ignorant*? That's an awfully big word for a little lady. Why ignorant?" I said

"Because cussing just means you're too lazy or stupid to use a better word. Like poop instead of *shit*."

"Or *crap* or *turd*?" I asked.

"Or *feces*," Tony said.

"Ahhh, I hate that word. It sounds disgusting," I said.

"Sit up and see if you're dizzy," Heather said. We helped Tony sit up and checked out the back of his head. A massive knot was forming at the point of impact.

"Man, you got a knot the size of Kansas on your head. I should pee on it."

"You're a crazy bastard. Stay away from me. Why in the world would you pee on me?"

"To sterilize your wound, keep you from getting an infection. It's a scientific fact. I read it in a magazine."

"In what magazine are you supposedly reading all this garbage?" Heather asked.

"*Boys' Life.*"

"Oh, please, they don't talk about that kind of stuff. Help me stand up," Tony said.

Once he was standing, Heather took a closer look at the knot on his head. "It's definitely big. Here..." And she kissed it, shocking me. That was the first kiss that any of us had shared. Wouldn't you know it, Tony was the beneficiary.

"What the hell was that?" I asked.

"I'm just trying to make it feel better. It's a scientific fact, read it in *Reader's Digest*," she replied.

"You don't know how to read. And *Reader's Digest* doesn't have those kinds of pictures," I said.

"Thanks, Heather, but I can feel the kiss already wearing off. Maybe you should do it again," Tony said.

"Don't press your luck, buster. Oh, and by the way, the run counted. Jake wins."

Yeah, Jake won, ha. I got the run, and he got the kiss. I didn't feel much like a winner.

4:20 p.m.
"I began to hit him, again and again..." Jake

My pew feels lonelier than it should as the church empties. Even though he hasn't been part of my life for the past twenty years, Tony was a cornerstone for the first twenty. I feel a deep sense of loss that surprises me given how little we've seen of each other recently. Plus I'm drowning in memories, both good and bad. My entire childhood is flashing past me. I'm flipping through long-forgotten memories like I flip channels on a TV: indiscriminately and rapidly. I instantly think of getting a drink. But I know that's not a good idea.

"Jake, thanks for coming."

I look up and feel my blush coming on. Heather is dressed in black. Black is a great color on her. Her brown hair is cut much shorter than when she visited me at the office. And her blue eyes sparkle even though they're a bit red from crying. It takes all of my self-control to not wrap my arms around her. I want to hold her tight, comfort her. That's what I tell myself anyway. The reality is I want to hold her for me. "You're truly twisted, lusting over a widow on the day that her husband is planted in the ground," my little angel says. "He's not sick; he's a red-blooded man. That's a healthy part of his genetics," my little devil responds.

"Heather, this must be tough." Damn, I sound like a dweeb. I stand and face her. She moves forward and wraps her arms around me. Her smell flashes through my senses, bringing back images, memories, and raw emotions. Her skin is still the smoothest thing I've ever touched in my life.

She steps back, smiles, and wipes her nose with a tissue. "Thank you, Jake. I've just been, I don't know, *unfocused* is the best description. Between talking with the police and figuring out finances, I don't know up from down."

"You look pretty amazing. I wanted to mention it earlier, but I thought it might sound wrong."

"It can never sound wrong coming from you, Jake."

Someone calls to her, telling her it's time to go. "Okay, I'll be right there," she calls over her shoulder and then says back to me, "Thanks for saying it, Jake. Will you promise to stick around at the reception until we can speak? I need some help on something. Please promise."

"Sure, I've got nowhere to be. I'll be the one closest to the bar when you're ready."

"Thanks, Jake." She squeezes my hands and turns and walks away. She joins a group and exits the church. How can I still be so connected to that amazing walk; is she doing that on purpose?

I remember our first kiss. It was when we were in high school and a few months after her and Tony's kiss on the baseball field. My family lived in a thousand-square-foot two-bedroom, one-bath home. There was zero privacy. At the time my parents were having their ups and downs. My dad had chosen to self-medicate with alcohol. One night during a loud verbal debate, he began pushing my mom around. It angered me. I was at that age when adrenaline would suddenly explode through me, and I'd react. No thinking required. I stepped between my parents and told Dad to leave Mom alone. I quickly discovered that he wasn't in the mood for my emotional growth. He slapped me hard and fast across my face.

I was stunned. My cheek stung but not nearly as much as my pride. My little devil rose up in fury. "Hit him. Hit him hard. He can't do that to you." I began to hit him, again and again, trying to utterly destroy this man. I wanted to reduce him to a pleading puddle of shame. After my first swing caught my dad on the mouth, he tried to grab my arms. But I was having nothing to do with that. So he just pulled his arms in close to protect himself. He was able to block most of my punches, letting them fall until I was too tired to swing anymore. When I stopped, he put his arms around me. "I'm sorry, Jake, I shouldn't have hit you. Please, Jake, I'm so, so sorry. I'm ashamed of myself, Jake. Please, believe me, I feel horrible. I'll never do it again."

I was young and emotionally charged. I broke out of my dad's embrace and stared angrily at him. It didn't register at the time, but later when I calmed down, I realized he had been crying. In that moment, though, I decided I needed some distance, so I stormed out of the house. I wandered around the neighborhood, feeling the worst I had in my short life. Every muscle in my body was tensed and ready to destroy something, anything. But as I walked, the emotion wore down. Back then, when I was upset, I'd run or walk off the emotion. Today, I've substituted liquor. My anger and hurt shifted to a sense of loneliness. I felt disconnected from all other people for the first time. My relationship with my parents changed forever that day. I think the separation that occurred was, to a degree, a healthy and normal part of growing up. A fistfight with my dad just probably wasn't the best way to implement the change.

Eventually I wandered to Heather's house. I hesitated before knocking on her door; I was still digesting the fact that she had kissed Tony. But I decided that I needed someone to talk to, and she had always been there for me in the past. She came outside, and we sat on a curb as the sky darkened. I told her what had happened and almost began to cry. She looked at my face and kissed me just to the side of my mouth. I looked into her eyes and sensed love and compassion, things I thought I had lost forever earlier in the evening. And I wanted more. I kissed her on the lips. She separated her lips and shared her warmth with me for a moment before she broke away.

"Walk with me, Jake." She stood and held out her hand. I took it, feeling her warmth and comforting grip, and stood up next to her. Looking into her eyes, I wondered just how far we were going.

We walked for an hour or so, through a wooded area in the neighborhood. We found a secluded spot and embraced, kissing passionately. I placed my hand on her breast, and she pushed me away. "Not here, not now, not like this," she said.

"When?"

"Tonight, Jake, I want to be with you tonight. I've wanted to be with you for a long time—a few more hours isn't all that long."

"Hours? I was thinking 'tonight' started at five. That means now."

"Trust me, Jake, we don't want to rush. Tonight, when it's late and everyone is asleep. Can you sneak out and come to my house?"

She looked eager and anxious. I felt that my answer was as important to her as it was to me. She didn't have to wait long. "Sure, no problem," I said as casually as possible.

"Okay, be there at midnight. When you get there, wait outside my window. If I don't open it, the date is off. If it's open, come in but be quiet. You understand, Jake? You have to be quiet."

"I get it, Heather."

I walked Heather to her street and headed home. Mom was waiting up for me; Dad was out.

"Jake, baby, come here. Jake, I'm so proud of you for standing up for me. Your dad was wrong. He knows it. He's promised to get some help, and I think he means it. Please, Jake, give him a chance. Let him prove he can change."

At that moment the last thing I wanted to think about was that bastard. It shocked me that she was defending him after the way he had treated her. He'd been a bastard for months. Why in the world would she help him? But I knew my help was important to her. "Okay, I'll give him a chance, Mom—for you, not for him.

"Thank you, baby, it will be good. Wait and see." She hugged me, and I went to my room.

I lay in bed thinking about the earlier craziness and the potential of tonight. I couldn't stay still with Heather on my mind. I quietly paced my room, hoping I could hurry the clock along. There was no need to leave any sooner than ten minutes before midnight. Heather's house was only five minutes away. I sensed that the less time I spent sneaking around outside, the less were the chances I'd be caught. But pacing my small room—five steps, turn, five steps, turn, over and over—was almost as bad as restlessly sitting behind some bush. "She's worth the wait," my little angel said.

With twenty minutes to go, I quietly slipped out through my window and moved cautiously toward her house. At night, skulking about, the world felt different. It felt big and empty. I felt strong and agile. I moved briskly but carefully, trying as best as I could to keep within the moon shadows.

As I neared Heather's house, my heart began to race. The rustle of the wind in the maples and cherry trees sounded sinister. It felt as if the earth knew my dirty secret and was shaking its massive finger at me. But all I could think about was her window and what lay beyond. I prayed it would be open. And I desperately longed for Heather to be on the other side, waiting, wanting me as much as I wanted her.

I moved to her side yard and stopped in the moon shadow of a rhododendron. I eagerly examined her window. I was ten minutes early, but it was open. I debated waiting until midnight but decided that I wouldn't survive that long. My heart was going to explode. I moved gently to the window and pulled myself up so I could see inside. I feared that her dad would be waiting for me. That he'd grab me by the scruff of my neck and cage me. I could imagine him selling tickets to people to come see the sex-crazed boy. But what I saw was Heather standing in the middle of the room and staring back at me. She was smiling and dressed in a cotton nightgown. I pulled myself up and swung my legs through her window. I dropped to the floor and stood in front of her, unsure.

Neither of us said a word. She came to me and pulled my shirt over my head. I smelled her hair as she tossed my shirt to the floor. We embraced and began to gently kiss. Our kisses became more fevered as she loosened my belt buckle and my pants slipped to the floor. I removed my underwear while she lifted her nightgown over her head. There we stood, totally naked with a sliver of moonlight shining in and illuminating our skin. I was entranced by the sheen of her breasts as she breathed.

She pulled me close, and we began exploring each other. Her touch was electrifying. Her body moved toward my hand, begging for more. Before I knew it, we were on her bed, alternating between being on top of and beside each other. Each position led to discoveries and new pleasures. Our heat rose. We were lit candles, slowly melting into each other. Our flames danced for what seemed like five minutes. But it was actually hours. When we burned down, we lay on our sides facing each other. Her eyes reminded me of smoldering embers. As I looked into her soul, I found myself wanting more. I wanted to know something. I wanted to know what this all meant. I was confused by this new connection.

My brain quickly overloaded from all of this introspection, and I said, "I know what you're thinking."

"Really, what that might be?" she asked.

"How could you be so fortunate? I mean, how lucky are you?"

"Jake, someday I hope you learn how to talk to a woman. You're supposed to be telling me how amazing I am, how blessed *you* are. Admit it, Jake—I'm your first."

"Tell her she's your twenty-first," my little devil said. "Be honest here, Jake. You're surrounded by quicksand, and there's no rescue team," my little angel said.

"Yeah, you're my first."

She smiled and began to kiss me gently. Her hands caressed my back and neck. I mirrored her actions.

"I like honesty, Jake. Not everyone is like you. You're kinder than other people, never lose that." She looked away but not before I saw in her eyes a hurt that didn't make sense to me then. Now I recognize that as we live, we all suffer wounds. Not all of them heal quickly.

"Don't let anyone else know about this. I can't afford the hit to my reputation," I said.

She smiled and looked back at me. "Oh, I think your reputation would be fine if people knew what we did tonight. Probably wouldn't help mine, but you'd be okay. You know, Jake, things are different now. Do you feel it? We've crossed an invisible line. One that you can't see until it's already behind you. But I'm happy. How about you, Jake? Are you happy?"

"Of course I am. I've wanted to be with you for years, Heather. I never thought you felt the same way."

"I do, Jake, you're special. You'll always be special and important to me. Just like I'll be to you; you'll never forget this night, or me."

"That's awfully deep. How do you know? Maybe I've already forgotten. In fact I think I have. How about I go outside, jump back in, and we start over? I just want to be sure I've got my memory cells properly set."

"You're funny, and you're partly right. It's time to jump, but *stay* out the window. Bye, Jake."

She was right. I remember it like it happened last night. I can still smell her sweat, feel her soft hair, and see her beautiful blue eyes as if she were standing in front of me. I involuntarily reach out into empty space to touch her. But she's gone. I have looked for her over the years. Not really her, but someone just like her. I've never been able to match the combination of passion, lust, and emotion that I experienced in her bedroom. I'm still searching.

4:40 p.m.
"Tonic, with a twist..." Jake

I leave the church and walk to my Jeep Wrangler. This Jeep has been my trusted steed for the past twelve years and nearly one hundred thousand miles. I turn on the engine and the radio in time to hear Kenny Chesney singing about a woman who is akin to tequila, both of them poisoning his blood. It feels like it was written for me.

I light a cigarette, but instead of gripping it with my lips and sucking in its toxins as quickly as I can, I set it in the ashtray and let the smoke fill the space with calming, poisonous fumes. I've decided that it's time to make changes; though my friends would argue for drinking to take the honors, smoking is the first victim. But I don't see the need to go cold turkey; I'll just stick to secondhand smoke. I sit and watch the occasional car pass by as I try to regain control of my emotions. A dead friend, a still-beautiful first love, and a hosted bar are just too much to wrap my head around. As Kenny finishes his last note, I put the car in gear and navigate to the reception hall.

I feel like I've known Heather her entire life. I feel like we're both still living just above the poverty line, like when we were kids. Yet here I am walking into the Portland Golf Club for Tony's funeral reception. The place is old-money elegance. It is the work of artisans. It seems as if craftsmen tailored each piece of wood especially for each specific location. The white window frames and moldings, contrasted with warm gray walls and carpeting, are comforting. At one end of the room, massive windows allow natural light to soften the space and afford us a view of a spectacular golf course lined with old firs, cedars, and pines. God, I hate this game.

The crowd is thick. I find it hard to believe that anybody has this many friends. Heather is surrounded by well-wishers. True to my word, I head straight to the bar.

"Good evening, would you like something?"

I'm about to say, "Dirty gin martini, up," but I remember the sunset outside of Carl's home and my friends' voices. "Tonic, with a twist." One step at a time.

"You got it."

I turn and observe the crowd, classifying each person. I break them down into four categories. One, the kids who run around and laugh and holler and play. They've forgotten Tony, if they ever knew him. Two, the folks who showed up because they felt they had to and now can't wait to leave. Three, those who embrace sadness and work hard to be in the middle of it; they cluster around Heather and try to be involved with every task. Four, the true friends and family—Heather, Tony's mom and sister, Heather's mom, and others I don't know but recognize by their subtle indications of grief: a tear, a glance cast down to their hands, or a heartfelt hug with another grieving person. As I watch them and work on my faux cocktail, I find myself sliding from true friend to kid. I'm ready to run around and have some fun. I can only lament for so long. Sadness has always had an expiration date with me.

As the sadness dissipates, the void it's left is filled with memories of happier times with Tony and Heather. Precious moments spent doing very little but talking while listening to albums. I miss the quiet simplicity of those days.

And I feel a twinge of guilt. I resent the time Tony spent with Heather that I didn't.

Heather and I slept with each other on a Saturday night. Since we didn't have cell phones back then, we didn't sext each other the rest of the weekend. We didn't see each other again until the following Monday morning, just before school.

I was excited and anxious to see Heather, and I found her, with Tony, just outside of my first-period classroom. Tony was just a distraction now. He was a third wheel in my mind. As I walked up to them, Tony greased my quick slide to despair.

"So, how's the stud feeling? Probably feeling pretty good, am I right?" His smile was as painful as his words.

Heather punched him in the shoulder and said, "Shut up, you ass, I don't want the whole world to know. I didn't tell him, Jake. He figured it out by himself, and he won't let it go."

I looked at Tony in utter confusion. I had worried over the weekend that if Tony found out, he'd be upset. After all, I had just slept with our best friend. How did that not infuriate him? It would infuriate me. I looked closer. Tony placed his arm casually over Heather's shoulder. I began to recall moments in the past year when they had shared looks that I didn't understand. It dawned on me that they'd been together. They'd been together for a while. My little angel and devil yelled at me to hit him. But before I could begin pummeling Tony, the bell rang.

"Gotta run, buddy. We'll talk about this after school." He winked and walked away.

I watched his back move down the hall. From a great distance, I could hear Heather saying my name. I turned, and she was actually right beside me. She shifted her weight back. I felt every muscle in my body tense. "You've been with him, haven't you? You've been with him a lot and for a long time."

"Jake, come on, that's not important. Saturday is all that matters, right? We had fun, and we can have fun again. But yes, Tony and I have fun too. That shouldn't matter—we're all friends. It's okay, isn't it?" No, it wasn't. I looked at her and saw my cocktail of humiliation and anger reflected in her eyes. Without a single word from me, I'm sure she sensed that I was hurt. And I was hurt, beyond anything I've ever experienced.

The more I thought about it, the angrier I became. It wasn't right. I didn't want to share Heather—not with Tony, not with anyone. I watched her walk away slowly. Maybe she wanted to stay and talk but felt pressured by the school bell. How was it possible that we had been programmed to abandon important conversations with a bell, like Pavlovian dogs?

I fumed all through classes. Once I heard my fellow students laughing and knew it was at me. The teacher had asked me a question to which I had given the brilliant answer of, "Huh?" I didn't meet up with Heather and Tony after school. I didn't see them, except in passing, for two weeks. By then I had accepted the truth. We never spoke about that Saturday night again. And I never again visited her window.

I closed off. Without me to fight for Heather's attention, Tony had an open field. They grew closer in the void of my departed emotion. In college they became a couple, and I became a third wheel. They were constantly finding me dates. Many of them were disastrous, but I remember a few fondly. Shortly after college they married. I attended the wedding. Two weeks after they married, I enlisted. Ever since then I've tried to bury the memory of Tony's wink and Heather's nervous smile. But it's proven to be impossible.

As I finish my third near-cocktail, I feel an arm encircle my waist. I track the arm back to Heather's shoulder. She's smiling at me like when we were kids. The smile is infectious, and I wrap my arms around her.

"You ready to talk?" I ask. The crowd is down to just a dozen folks, most of whom are getting ready to leave.

"Yes, but not here. I'll go crazy if another person cries on my shoulder. Are you okay to drive?"

"Sure. Where do you want to go?"

"You choose."

I choose the Hall Street Grill in Beaverton. It's still proud of its '70s décor—original, not newly done—and feels comfortably warm. I'm intimate with the place. I dine here on many Monday nights when the bottled wine is half-price. We find a booth in back. I slide into the booth, and she slides in next to me instead of across the table.

"I need some warmth—are you okay with that?" Heather asks. It sounds like a question but it isn't. It's pure Heather. Our sides touch on the narrow bench, and I feel the old electricity—must be muscle memory.

"How you holding up?"

"Better, now that the funeral is over with. It seemed like we were on hold forever." She dabs the corner of her eye with a tissue. "The police needed to do an autopsy before we could cremate him."

"They catch the guy?"

"No, but they say they're still looking. I think they've given up but won't say so. All they really know is that the driver was speeding because of how badly Tony's body was damaged." She hesitates for a moment to regain her composure. "They think that he was in the street when he was hit. He was out jogging on a dark street wearing dark clothes. Sometimes I think he wanted to die." Heather tears up. I gently brush a drop from below her eye.

"Why do think he wanted to die?"

"Oh, I don't know, it was just a feeling. We had drifted apart, and he'd been...melancholy, I guess is the best way to describe him."

"I know it's painful and confusing right now, Heather. I miss him too. But dark clothes on a dark street isn't a suicide attempt. At worst, it's bad judgment."

"I know, I'm just mixed up inside." Heather looks at me. For a moment I can sense that she's searching for something, like one does for a misplaced earring, or a scarf. "Jake, you remember that night, that one night?"

I look at her, stunned. "Ask her what night she's referring to," my little devil says. "Tell her kinda-sorta," my little angel says. "Yeah, like it was yesterday," is what I say.

She smiles. "Me too. I've thought about it a lot. Sometimes I cry because I chose Tony instead of you. But that's not entirely true, is it? I chose both of you, and you chose to close off. You did that, you know. You never really got angry about things—you just got quiet."

"My dad was a yeller; I just never saw the value. I find a whisper and a look can convey more information more clearly and quickly. Be afraid of whisperers. Yellers are just toothless bullies." I remember my recent altercation with Grizzly Adams and Jeffrey the bartender. I wasn't much of a whisperer, and it embarrasses me.

"Whisper to me now, Jake."

I look at her, lean in, and kiss her softly. She reaches up and holds my head in place as we taste the past.

I move away, still looking at her. Is she testing me? Or is she just lonely? "We better be careful or someone might think we conspired to knock Tony off," I say.

"I'm not worried about what people think. You know that, though, don't you?"

"That's always been part of your charm."

"Or demise, on occasion." Her eyes focus on a different place and time. "It's just a kiss. It isn't a promise of life ever after. A kiss between old lovers." She looks back at me, and smiles. "Jake, as much as I'd like to see how well we can reenact the past, that's not what I want to talk to you about."

“I figured as much.”

“I need to hire you. After I told you about Tony, our attorney gave me a key to a safety-deposit box. It was Tony’s box; I didn’t know he had it. I went to the bank, opened it, and found three things. There was a leather pouch, an envelope, and a gun. A loaded gun—another thing I didn’t know he owned. I opened the leather pouch and found diamonds inside. I think the diamonds frightened me as much as the gun. I couldn’t imagine why Tony had diamonds or how he obtained them. Anyway, I left the gun and the pouch in the box. But I took the envelope.” She looks down at her purse, pulls a white envelope from it, and hands it to me.

On the outside it says, *Hey, baby, take this to Jake.* I look at her.

“I didn’t open it. Nobody knows about it but us,” she says.

“Do you have any idea what might be inside?” I ask.

“Not a clue.”

“Well, I doubt there’s a bomb, so I might as well open it.”

“Might as well. Do you want me to leave?”

“No. No secrets.” I examine the outside of the envelope and don’t see any other markings. I tear it open. Inside are a piece of paper and a flash drive. Damn, I hate flash drives. Flash drives mean big secrets. I pull out the piece of paper, and Heather and I read at the same time.

Jake,

You’re still a loser, although if you’re reading this, I’m dead or in jail. Either way, I’d still rather be me. Just kidding, buddy.

Over the past few years, I’ve gathered some insurance on some business partners. Only they take business real serious, if you get my drift. I've warned them that if anything happens to me, I'll take them down. That's what the flash drive is for. I need you to be the ghost of Tony and seek vengeance.

But more importantly, protect Heather. She could be at risk.

Catch you in the afterlife,
Tony

PS I know what you're thinking; keep your mitts off of her.

I look at Heather, who looks truly frightened. "Don't worry, Heather. I'll touch you if you want me to."

She laughs and says, "It's nice to know you haven't changed." But the comic relief doesn't last long. She looks at me anxiously. "I'm frightened, Jake. Tony was killed and I find a secret safety-deposit box with things I would never have guessed he'd have. He never mentioned any of this to me. Am I in danger?"

I want to give her a sugarcoated answer. But I'm afraid she may be resistant to what has to happen if I'm not blunt. "Yes, I think you could be in danger. I thought he was an architect?"

"He was. This is a complete surprise to me. What could he have possibly been involved with?"

"I don't know, but it was probably illegal. He told the nasty guys that he was holding information that could burn them. He was nervous enough to hoard diamonds and a gun. You'll be the first person his business partners look to for the insurance. They've probably been watching you ever since Tony was killed."

The realization strikes her, and her eyes grow wide. "Damn it, Tony, what did you do? Do you think he was murdered?"

"Not necessarily. It could have been an accident. But the bad guys aren't going to care; they're going to be afraid that the flash drive might become public. We have to assume they're going to contact you."

"Jake, I don't have the ability to deal with this. What do I do? Oh my God..."

I'm touched that he'd trust Heather's safety to me. I'm angry that he'd do something so stupid that my protection became necessary. "Heather, do you trust me? I mean trust me with your safety, maybe even your life?"

"Yes, I do."

"Then you need to listen to me. I need you to do exactly what I tell you to do when I tell you to do it. If you don't, you could be at risk. Are you okay with that?"

"Yes, thank you, Jake. What do I do?"

"First, you'll need to go to a safe location. You won't be able to go back home until we figure this out. You'll give me a list of items you need to live for two weeks, and my assistant, Sarah, will gather them for you. Second, you are no longer going to make phone calls—to anyone. If you want to make one last call to someone to set up a story so people aren't worried, do it now."

"I should probably call my mom. I'll tell her I'm going out of town. She can answer everyone else's questions."

"How about work?" I ask. "You should probably let your boss know you're going to be away for a while."

"Actually, I haven't worked in over a year. I quit my job

because Tony was making good money. He told me I didn't need to be in a hurry to find another job. So I haven't hurried."

"Okay, call your mom. As soon as you're done, I'm confiscating your phone. From now on you can't make a call or get on a computer without my approval. There's a possibility that if you do, someone will trace you. Do you understand?"

"Oh, come on, Jake, I..."

"You're either all of the way in or I can't help you."

"Okay, okay. Let me call my mom."

"Tell her you need some time to think. You'll be gone for a week or so, and you'll check back with her in a couple of days."

While she talks to her mom, I call Sarah and give her instructions. I ask her to meet us. Before she comes in, she's to scan the parking lot for observers. Heather finishes her call, and I take her phone. I open it, take out the SIM card, and put the pieces into my pocket.

We sip our drinks and try to keep the conversation light while we wait for Sarah. I'd start quizzing her for more important info, but someone could be eavesdropping.

My phone rings; it's Sarah. "Yeah."

"I'm outside. I don't see anyone casing the parking lot, but I found a tracer on your car. What do you want me to do?"

I cup my hand around my mouth and the phone. "Leave the tracer, for now. Don't come in. I'll text you a list of stuff that Heather needs, and we'll wait here for you. Don't go back to her place—may not be safe. Buy new. When you get back, bring your car around to the back of the restaurant and park. Leave the keys under the driver's seat. Come in through the front door and sit near the rear exit so you can watch the crowd as Heather and I walk out the back. If someone jumps up, try to follow them. But don't take any chances. If they spot you, turn and run. You got it?"

"Check: turn and run."

"When the coast is clear, take the Jeep—you know where the spare key is. Make sure you dump the tracer. Park somewhere and grab a cab and meet us at the Phoenix Inn out by 217 and Kruse Way. We'll be under the names Mr. and Mrs. Jesse Smith. The manager knows me, and he'll do an all-cash, off-the-books deal. Oh, and better get some burners, just in case. We'll be ready as soon as you get back."

"Okay."

As I hang up, Heather says, "That sounds like world-class espionage."

I put my hand on her face and shift closer as if we're going to kiss and whisper to her, "Heather, if these guys are that quick to put a tracer on my car, we have to assume they know what they're doing. We don't take any chances from now on. This is serious stuff. You have to do what I say."

"I get it, Jake. You're freaking me out, but I get it. What do we do now?"

"Type your list of what you need into my phone." I go back to people watching while Heather types, and types and types some more. "How long does it take to type *underwear*, *toothbrush*, and *toothpaste*?" my little devil asks. "Can I see?" I ask her.

"Sure, but I'm not—"

"Hypoallergenic pillows?" I read further. "You have more cosmetics than clothes listed. Heather, we need to streamline this."

"Jake, you're not a woman—you don't understand. I need these things. I need—"

"Heather, basics on this list; we can make a second run later."

She looks away and shakes her head like I'm an idiot or, worse, a man. When she turns back, her eyes say I'm crazy.

"How about underwear—is that basic or optional?" she asks, smiling deviously.

"Well..."

She shakes her head and sighs. "Never mind, I'll trim it down. What do we do after I'm done with my *abbreviated* list?"

"We order more food, laugh, and act as casual as we can."

She finishes the list, and Sarah sends me a text saying it will take a couple of hours to get it all. I text her back and ask her to get only the items necessary for tonight. We'll work on the rest later.

Next, I call a buddy who manages the Phoenix Inn south of town and arrange to get a room off the books.

Over the next sixty minutes, we pretend to be old flames while we watch for any watchers. We briefly touch on my divorce from Sue. I tell her how hurt I was and how I still feel like I failed her. I nurse a single glass of red wine. My daily limit, I've decided, until I know I have things under control. Eventually Sarah calls and announces that she's about to walk into the restaurant.

I see her out of the corner of my eye as she walks past and sits at an empty table next to the entrance to the kitchen. I've been through the kitchen before. It's a great way to escape a tail or a wannabe fighter.

"We're up. Don't look at anybody; just keep up with me. You ready?"

"Do I have a choice?"

"Not a good one."

We slide out of the booth and casually walk toward Sarah. As we pass her, I see her inquisitive blue eyes over the top of her menu, switching between an examination of Heather and the other patrons. We move into and through the kitchen to the back door. In the kitchen we ignore a few questioning stares, but no one tries to stop us. Outside we jump into Sarah's car and pull away, blending with traffic. For the first ten minutes, I drive in random directions, looking for a tail. I cut through a couple of parking lots at a quick pace, studying the world behind me through my rearview mirror. I don't see anyone matching my herky-jerky driving, so I merge back into traffic and head to the hotel.

We grab Sarah's purchases from the backseat, check into the hotel, and settle into a room on the fourth floor of the Phoenix Inn. The room is a white box with standard mass-produced hotel décor. It has one double window facing the freeway and office buildings, two queen beds, and a separate sitting area with two chairs and a table. Heather hasn't said a word since the restaurant. That's a record for her. But a dead husband with secrets and the risk of personal harm tend to change a person's demeanor.

We sit in chairs. "We should be good here. Sarah will be here in the next hour if all goes well. Right now, we need to have a talk—a long talk. I need to know everything you can tell me about Tony, including your personal life. This may not be comfortable, but I'll only ask for information that is important." I hold her hands, and she looks at me. "I know how hard it can be to talk openly about your marriage. I just went through a verbal cavity search by the attorneys in my divorce. But you have to be completely open with me. Don't try to downplay or hold back anything. Do you understand, Heather?"

"Sure, no secrets, no holding back. I'm ready."

"Let's start with Tony. I know he was an architect. Tell me about his professional life and his hobbies."

Heather narrates for about fifteen minutes. He was a partner at a moderate-sized firm that handles both residential and commercial projects. He worked long hours and often spent nights at his office. He played poker with buddies twice a month. He was an avid golfer. And when he was at home, he'd disappear into a book. I see frustration on her face. I remember my uncomfortable silences with Sue, how we could be in the same house without inhabiting the same space.

"I used to think that TV was addictive. But when he was into a book, he could be sitting next to me and not be there. The last few years it was getting worse. I know you're going to ask, and no, I wasn't happy, and I don't think he was either. We'd grown apart, and it felt like we were just going through the motions." Heather tears up. "Oh, I'm so angry that I cry over him. I'm so mixed up, Jake. I'm angry that he ignored me. At the same time I miss him. I don't know what to feel. And then I'm afraid I don't feel enough. I'm just all mixed up."

I hug her. "It's okay to be confused. Hell, Sue just moved to a new address, and I'm still sorting through all of the emotions." She smiles and dries her tears. "I hate to ask, Heather, but do you think he was cheating on you?" My little angel and my little devil are both indignant. "This lovely person couldn't have killed her husband?" my little angel asks. "Ask her if she's got a butler," my little devil says.

She subtly shifts away from me, and her breath catches. "I don't know. He had in the past. He apologized when I found out then and said it wouldn't happen again. But...well, we hadn't been intimate for quite a while. We share...shared the same bed, but we were like two strangers trapped in the last available hotel room near the airport when all the planes are grounded. We slept at the edges of the bed with our backs to each other and no warmth in between."

She stands and moves to look out the window at nondescript two- and three-story buildings across the freeway, with I-5 traffic whooshing past. I hear her take a deep breath and see her nod, as if she's accepted a new truth. She turns and looks at me with hurt in her eyes. "Jake, I'm more angry then sad. He was keeping secrets, and now it looks like he got himself killed."

I walk to her. I wrap my arm around her shoulders, and she leans into my embrace. I catch the scent of her hair—it reminds me of when we were kids in the moonlight. Thoughts of that long-ago moment spring into my brain, and I'm tempted to lose myself, to kiss her, to tear her clothes off. "Jesus, Jake, she's a widow," my little angel says. All I hear from my little devil is a chuckle.

I move away. I need to ask questions, and I can't concentrate while I'm physically close to her. "I have to ask, Heather—were you cheating on him?"

Pain floods her eyes. She stares at me for a moment and then looks down at her folded hands and whispers a simple, soft no.

9:13 p.m.
"These are dangerous people who'll take any action necessary..." Sarah

Sarah arrives carrying laptops and cell phones. She sets them on the table and walks to Heather and shakes her hand.

"It's a pleasure to meet you, Heather. Jake has spoken of you fondly."

"It's nice to meet you too, Sarah. I can't thank you enough for helping me."

I notice a coolness in both of them as they examine and categorize each other. My little angel says that's a natural step toward building a trusting friendship. My little devil thinks that they both think they own a piece of Jake, and they're making sure the other knows it.

"Oh, it's just part of the job, right, Jake?" Sarah asks.

"Right. What happened at the restaurant after we left?"

"A male diner tried to follow you through the kitchen. He reentered the dining area after a few seconds and jogged out through the front. I watched from inside the restaurant as he searched the parking lot. He approached your Jeep and confirmed the tracer was still in place. Then he got in a parked black Toyota. He remained there for approximately fifteen minutes before he drove away.

"I went to the Jeep and removed the tracer. I put it on

a tree limb and drove the Jeep to a rental agency. They'll store the Jeep on their back lot until we return the rental."

"Perfect; power up your laptop."

"Sure," she says. Sarah and I sit next to each other at the table while Heather wanders over to one of the beds.

I hand the thumb drive to Sarah. "Let's see what's on this."

Heather stares at the tiny drive as Sarah plugs it into the computer. She punches a few buttons, pauses, then hits a few more. "Okay, there's not all that much here. It looks like some pictures, some PDFs, and one Word document. The Word doc is titled *Notes*. Let's start there." She double-clicks on an icon.

"The first page is a summary, and the rest of the fifteen pages are dates and notes, with what appear to be references to the PDFs and pictures. Let me have a few seconds to skim through."

As Sarah reads, I walk over to Heather. "You okay?"

"I don't know. We're about to find out what might have gotten Tony killed. The drive looks like a gun to me." I put my hand on her shoulder but return to the table as Sarah begins to speak again.

"The quick and dirty of it seems to be that Tony's firm was fronting for a criminal group. They were negotiating sweetheart deals with the city for construction projects. It looks like there were bribes and coercion involved. Based upon his notes, these are dangerous people who'll take any action necessary to protect themselves."

As I read along with Sarah, I begin to get a chill. "I recognize some of these names. These are not men to trifle with. Sarah, why don't you focus on doing a workup on the names on the list."

"Okay..." Sarah is giving me a look, but I ignore it.

I look over to Heather, who is looking down at the floor. "Does his narrative talk about the diamonds?"

"Let me see. Yes, they're his getaway cash. He says there's about a million in street value in the bag. He bought them with his share of the loot," Sarah says and then looks up at Heather, who is ashen.

Heather looks at me. "Jake, you have to believe I didn't know anything about this, nothing at all."

"I do."

"Do you think they killed Tony?"

"I don't think so. They wouldn't risk surfacing the information. No, I think the men on the thumb drive had too much to lose to kill Tony."

"Maybe they just think it will be easier to get the information from Heather," Sarah says.

"Possibly, but they're taking a risk. What if Tony had set things up so that the attorney just mailed the thumb drive to the police instead of giving a safety deposit key to Heather? No, something else is going on here. I don't know what yet, but we need to find out."

"What do we do now?" Heather asks.

"Sarah and I are going to review the information. You're going to watch TV, or sit over in that chair and watch us read. The less you know, the better off you'll be."

"How about I go find some food while you start your review of the files," Sarah says.

Heather and I aren't hungry, so Sarah leaves with an order for one. The computer is sitting in front of me, but I can't concentrate on digitized documents. All I can think about is Heather sitting ten feet away. I pretend to focus on the computer screen, but I sense she's staring at me. I glance in her direction and confirm my suspicion. "I can't work with you staring at me."

"There's plenty of time for work." She stands and walks over to me. She puts her hand behind my head and bends down to kiss me. Her soft lips caress mine, then my eyelid, then the base of my ear. My eyes close as my cells spark where she makes contact.

"What the hell, Jake. You just melt for any ol' dame?" my little angel asks. "Well, yeah," my little devil answers. But she isn't any ol' dame. She's Heather, my first love.

"How long until Sarah's back?"

"Not long, forty-five minutes, maybe an hour."

"Jake, I hope you'll stay here tonight. I need you. Is that terrible? Tony's been dead for two weeks, and all I can think about is you." She begins her soft caress again. I stand and move one hand to her hair as my other wraps around her back. She looks at me, waiting for my answer.

"No, it's not terrible," I finally answer her.

"Jake, now you concentrate on that computer. Later you're mine."

I watch her hips sway all the way back to the bed, ten monstrous feet away, ten feet between the woman of my childhood dreams and me. She looks back at me and smiles, sits, and turns on a meaningless TV show with mundane acting and a boring script. I recognize it because I watch it every week. I turn back toward the laptop and pretend to read.

10:00 p.m.
"Tonight will be my last night…" Heather

Sarah returns for her laptop. She's decided that she can accomplish more if she can find a quiet space to be by herself. Before she leaves, we step out into the hallway.

"Did you get anything more from the drive?" Sarah asks.

"No, nothing but support for the notes that you read."

"Did you even look at the laptop? I mean, maybe you were distracted."

"Sarah, it's not what you think. Heather's from my past. She's a client."

Sarah laughs, practically doubling over. "From your past—you're killing me." Just as quickly as she began to laugh she stops. "Don't bullshit me, Jake. You're smitten."

"Smitten? I don't even know what that means. And stop making this about me. Can we focus on what's important? Thank you. To be safe, don't use your cell—use one of the burners. Oh, and stay away from the office for now." Even though Sarah knows how to take care of herself, I still worry about her.

She lets me know that she'll be at her sister's instead of her place. "Jake, don't worry. I'll be fine. We're pretty big targets, aren't we?"

"Yes, maybe, but we have options."

"Like what?"

"Our first option is to take the info to the bad guys, give it to them, and beg them not to kill us. Our second option is to go to the police and live in witness protection for the rest of our lives. I'm hoping that somewhere in this stuff there's a third option; one that gets us out from the middle. But we won't know until we've finished going through the files. We have to have an answer and choose a strategy pretty quickly or someone will decide for us. I don't think that will play out to our advantage."

"Are you spending the night?" she asks like it's a casual question, but I sense there's more to it. Sarah clearly doesn't approve of Heather. Actually, it's not Heather—I think it's Heather and me together that bothers her. My guess is she's right again. But there's a side of me that doesn't care.

I look at the room door and then back at Sarah. "Yeah, I don't think it's smart to leave Heather alone."

"That's funny; I was thinking it would be smart for you to leave her alone. Being romantic with a client can get people hurt. You know that, Jake. Plus, she's been a widow for what, two, three seconds?"

"It's been that long? That's a relief—now I'm not so worried about impressions. Sarah, I hear what you're saying. I'll be cool."

She laughs and says, "Right. Get divorced, get thrown in jail, drink like a fish. You're a real cool cucumber. This is a bad idea. I know you're tired of hearing me harp on this Jake, but you need to be careful. Heather is going through a lot of emotional trauma; you don't want to be the rebound guy. You know that guy; he's the knight on a steed? Spoiler alert: he always gets trampled by the end of the book."

"Jake, buddy ol' pal, there are worse things than being a rebound stud," my little devil snickers.

I hesitate a second to keep from biting Sarah's head off. She's concerned; it's etched all over her face. I take a deep breath as I look anywhere but at Sarah. When I turn to her, I say, "Thank you. I know you're trying to protect me."

She smiles and gives me a quick hug. Leaning back into the room, she says, "Bye, Heather. Get some rest. I suspect we're going to be busy tomorrow."

"Bye, Sarah. It's good to meet you. And thank you for helping me. I know it puts you at risk as well. I can't thank the two of you enough."

Sarah waves and turns so I can read her lips as she walks out the door: *Oh, I'll bet you'll find a way to thank Jake.* It was either that or, *Oh, I'll pick up your dry cleaning, Jake.* I'll get clarification tomorrow.

Back inside the room, I sit on the bed. I look at Heather, who's sporting a stunning smile that seems full of promise. She still looks lovely in her funeral attire: an all-black dress with buttons down the front. She's barefoot and isn't wearing nylons. Her legs are long and slender. Her eyes are sparkling with mischief. We look at each other for a few seconds, and then she begins to casually unbutton her dress.

"Heather, as much as I want this to happen, you're a client and we have to be careful. I don't want you more at risk than you are already. I don't want my professional judgment clouded by a personal relationship."

"I don't need your professional judgment at the moment."

"But you will, eventually. There are bad guys out there."

"Sounds like I'm in grave danger." Her dress falls to the floor.

"No, you're not in grave danger. More like moderate danger, with tabasco sauce."

"Um, so, maybe 'tonight will be my last night on earth' kind of danger?" Her slip hits the dress.

"No, of course not. You'll be fine."

"But you're not sure, are you?" She crosses the room and places a finger on the light switch. She turns and looks at me, daring me to stop her.

"I'm sure. Heather..."

She flips the switch, casting the room in darkness. I hear her pad over to me. She pulls me to my feet and begins to undress me. I'm powerless to stop her. But surprisingly I find the power to help her finish her own undressing. I want this. I want her.

We fall onto the bed skin-to-skin and eyelash-to-eyelash. We caress with no limits. My body heats up, and slowly we begin to move in rhythm. As the rhythm quickens, I see the teenage girl in the moonlight. I can hear the wind outside her window, I can see her moonlit room, and I can smell her then and now. We slow and lie facing each other. I can't see her expression in the darkness, but I imagine her smile. She turns away from me, and we spoon as we drift off to sleep.

Monday, July 25

9:00 a.m.
"I think the thieves were stealing from the crooks..." Sarah

The next morning Sarah arrives just as I'm exiting the bathroom. I'm dressed and ready for business. She looks at the two queen beds and instantly recognizes that one was not slept in. I had tried to make the used bed look unused, but obviously I missed a fold or two. "Why didn't you mess up the second bed instead of making the first bed?" my little angel asks.

How did I fall into this space between Heather cuddling up to me on one side and Sarah poking me with a stick on the other? Sarah shakes her head slightly and looks at me like I'm a moron. "Hey, she works for you. She can't look at you like that," my little devil says. "Yeah, stand up to her. Of course, she'll probably break you like a matchstick if you do," my little angel says. I decide to ask, "Hey, sweetheart, are those donuts for me?"

"Right, just for you; I'm sure you're awfully hungry."

Before I can respond, Heather says, "Oh, he is, aren't you, tiger?"

Sarah turns red. As Heather turns to check out the donut selection, Sarah looks at me and quietly growls. Then out loud she asks, "Are you two going to be at each other from now on?" That's Sarah, straight to the punch line.

I say no at the same instant that Heather says yes. We look at each other; Heather smiles at me and turns back to the donuts. I look at Sarah and sense that Heather's name is on her naughty list, right below mine.

I mouth, *Stop it*, to her. She nods toward Heather and mouths, *You stop it*, back to me. Or maybe, it was, *Mmm, donuts*.

Heather breaks our mime communication. "You guys can speak out loud if you want. I'm a big girl." I look at Heather, and she smiles and winks. I look back at Sarah, and her eyes burn a hole in my head.

"Did you dig any more info from the drive?" I ask Sarah.

"Actually, I did. Come look at this." She retrieves her laptop and powers it on.

While we wait, I see just how pretty she is when she's angry. Her intense blue eyes exude more emotion than I anticipated. Heather has definitely made an impression. I don't recall Sarah being territorial in the past. I've seen her angry, sad, happy, but not this. This is new.

"Here are a series of executed contracts Brown Construction won, no bid. Tony's firm managed each of them and did all of the admin, including billing and collecting from the city. Here is the management agreement between Tony's firm and the construction company. It says that Tony's group is to retain 10 percent of the gross, with the remainder going to Brown. And here are the actual payments that were made to the construction company. Notice anything?"

"The payments to the construction company look like they're less than 90 percent."

"Exactly: I think the thieves were stealing from the crooks. I estimate as much as fifty thousand on just these four contracts. It looks like there are over a hundred contracts here. This could be a really big number."

"Are you saying that Tony was a crook?" Heather asks.

I imagine that, emotionally, she's spiraling down. I want

to give her a hug or squeeze her hand, but Sarah may amputate my arm if I do so.

Sarah looks at Heather and seems to soften a bit. “Yes, it does look that way,” she says. “It looks like his firm was illegally obtaining contracts from the city and not paying everything it owed to Brown Construction. The flash drive proves he knew about all of it, and the diamonds pretty strongly suggest that he was benefitting from it.”

Heather nods and turns away.

“Can you see who had the sticky fingers?”

“Tony’s partner signed all of the checks to the construction company. But that doesn’t mean Tony wasn’t involved. He had the contracts—he could have done the math. He doesn’t mention it in his summary, but why have the management contract on the thumb drive if he didn’t intend it to be discovered?”

“Do we know who owns Brown Construction?”

“Sammy Bahn.”

Jesus, Tony was doing business with Sammy “Knuckles” Bahn. Sammy is an old-school badass from a Vegas syndicate. He worked his way up the food chain through violence, knocking off so many of his bosses that his bosses’ bosses started leaving town. Sammy doesn’t break knuckles anymore. Now he hires associates to handle that sort of thing, and he is not a patient guy. If you get on his bad side, you best get back to his good side or get all your sides out of town.

“You’re sure? I thought he was in Vegas? What’s he doing in Portland?”

“Dead sure.”

“I suppose that’s better than just plain dead. Are you done with the background checks on the list on the thumb drive?”

"Pretty much. I need a little bit more time."

"Okay, when you're done with that, start a background check on Tony, Tony's partner, and their firm. We need to get as much info as possible. I'll go to Milt and try to find out what the police know about Tony's death. You stay here with Heather while I'm out with Milt." I look over to Heather, who still looks unsettled. "I won't be long, and Sarah's armed. You'll be safe."

Heather nods and offers a weak smile.

"I need to speak to you in the hall for a moment," Sarah says quietly.

"Heather, Sarah and I need to step outside for a moment. She'll be back in five." I grab my coat, hug Heather, and squeeze her hand.

"What?" I ask Sarah when we are in the hall.

"Well?"

"Well what? You called this meeting."

"You're off your game. You're being influenced by your love affair with the ghost of childhood past. You need to let me run this investigation."

"I don't know what you're talking about. I mean, I know what you mean about Heather and me, but how is my head not clear?"

"You told me a long time ago that only a dead detective trusts his client. Yet you didn't ask me to do a workup on Heather. I thought maybe you didn't want her to overhear, but you didn't even text me the request. I think it's more than that. You're out over your tips. I'm doing a workup on her, and you're going to stay out of the way."

"I said that dead detective thing?"

"Yes."

"Huh. I was right, of course. Sure, do the check on her. In fact"—I reach into my coat pocket and pull out the pieces of Heather's phone—"start with her phone."

"Okay, here are the keys to the rental."

"Are you okay hanging out here?"

"Why wouldn't I be?"

My little devil asks, "Does every question have to be a fight?"

"Well, it seemed that maybe you and Heather weren't getting along so well. I just wanted to make sure. I don't want to be one of those insensitive bosses."

"Oh, you're a *sensitive* boss now. Heather and I are fine. My problem is that I can see that you're Humpty Dumpty, she's the wall, and I'm all the king's men. Want me to tell you how the story ends?" She looks at me like she's running through being concerned, frustrated, and pissed off. I suspect she'll spend time at each stop.

"Sarah, I appreciate you, you know that. And I know I've got some issues to deal with—"

"Oh my God, some issues? You're a garbage bag full of issues. Jesus, go meet with Milt, and I'll babysit your dreamboat."

10:50 a.m.
"I'm here to see the snake charmer..." Jake

The rental is a blue and gold, foreign, economy-class tissue box on wheels. I get in and feel like a big gorilla in a tiny cage. I can't set the driver's seat far enough back to get comfortable leg room, and I'm going to have to steer with my belly. Not that my belly is all that big. Well, it's bigger than it should be, but it's not like I'm packing a pony keg under my shirt. More like a six-pack with foam insulation.

I drive down Highway 217 to the Canyon Road exit and make my way to Milt's Laundromat empire. He recently inherited a chain of Laundromats and dry cleaning stores that throw off enough cash that he doesn't have to work as a cop. Sometimes he even works at the store in Beaverton, where he tinkers with the machinery when he isn't hiding in his back office. He says he's back there doing paperwork, but I know he's just embarrassed by his horrific wardrobe.

I park the clown car and enter the store. It never ceases to amaze me how big a change I feel when I walk through that door. Outside are fresh air, a warm breeze, and the sounds of traffic. Inside the air is filled with particles from dress shirts and blouses dancing to the squeaks of machinery and bursts of steam. A young girl stands at the counter with the caterpillar of plastic-wrapped clothes behind her. Her brown eyes are the same color as her hair. She's wearing jeans and a crop top that emphasizes her developing womanhood.

"I'm here to see the snake charmer. Is Milt handcuffed to a heater back there, or can he spare a couple of minutes?"

"I'll check." She smiles and disappears into the hanging plastic bags of clothing. A minute later I hear rustling, and Milt emerges. As expected, he's wearing clothes that likely were rejected by homeless people.

"Aw, shit. What do you want? Who's trying to kill you now?" he asks.

"Oh, come on, Milt. I'm not that guy. I came over to collect the twenty you owe me from poker. You know, from the hand where I kicked your ass. Ha-ha."

"You said we could square up at the next game."

"I'm teasing. Someone may be trying to kill me, and I need your help."

Milt grins. "It'll cost you twenty."

"Deal."

We walk into the back and sit at his tiny desk in his tiny office. I'm convinced that he's a hermit at heart. He feels comfortable in small spaces that discourage visitors. His desk is cluttered with stock reports and investment statements. He's lectured me on the merits of saving for retirement and old age more times than I care to remember. I always ask him why I should save when I can just live with him.

"You look and sound better. Have you been drinking?"

I'm so glad I've given him another fault to focus on. "A couple of glasses of wine—I swear that's it. I'm guessing you guys have Sarah doing blood tests on me when I'm sleeping at my desk. She can attest to my effort."

"But that's not why you're here."

"No, that's not why I'm here. I need your help."

I give him the rundown on what has happened and what I'm concerned about. Actually, I don't tell him much. I don't tell him about the contracts with the city, Brown Construction, or Sammy. I don't want him giving too much info to his buddies. They might decide there's been a crime and mess up my survival strategy. I just tell him my history with Tony and Heather.

"But what I need from you is everything you can get on Tony's death."

"Hit-and-run, you say?"

"Yes, two weeks ago Sunday."

"Do you know what street he was on?"

"Somewhere in Southeast Portland, on or near Woodstock."

"Okay, hang on." He dials and listens. "Stevie, it's Milt. Sure, I'll be there. Yes, I'll be there. No...Stevie, I promise I'll be there. Hey, I need a favor. I have a buddy whose friend was killed in a hit-and-run a week ago yesterday. He wants some info. Can you help? Sure, I can hold." While he's holding, he fidgets with some stock reports on his desk. "Al Jenkins is the cop in charge. So, Jake, how much you setting aside each month?"

"Lots, tons, gallons, I'm expanding into a storage—"

"Yeah, that would be great. Thanks, Stevie." He puts his hand over the mouthpiece. "Stevie's transferring me to Al. 'Hi, Al, did Stevie tell you what this is about? Great, can you help me? Yes, that's the guy. Can you give me the rundown? Great, is it okay to put you on speaker? Jake Brand. Yes, that Jake Brand. Go ahead. '"

What the hell does *that* mean?

Milt looks at me. "We're on hold. He has to pull up the file."

"What the hell did *that* mean?" I ask.

"Well, you see, Jakey, when someone puts the phone down—"

"Not that—"

"I know. Listen, there aren't a lot of secrets around the station. You're infamous these days."

"Infamous is what I've been going for. Nice to be noticed for my—"

"Okay"—we hear from the phone—"Anthony Weintraub was struck down at approximately 10:00 p.m. on Southeast Tolman Street between Twenty-Eighth and Twenty-Ninth. There were minor skid marks but not like the driver was breaking. And there was some debris that may have come from the assailant's vehicle. If it is from the vehicle, we're looking for a Nissan Leaf. Based upon the damage done to the victim, we estimate that the driver had to be going over forty at impact. We don't have any witnesses. The victim was wearing dark clothing, so it's possible that he was close to invisible. But even if he were invisible, the driver was almost certainly speeding and left the scene. We want him.

"We've put out an APB for a smashed-up Nissan Leaf. We've contacted all of the repair shops within fifty miles. So far we haven't had any hits. The case is cool going to cold. Until we can find the car, we don't have anything to move on. Do you want a rundown on the injuries?"

"No, thanks," I say. I don't need to hear how badly my friend was damaged.

"Do you have any ideas on what might have happened, Mr. Brand?"

"No. Tony was one of my best friends when I was a kid. I told his wife I'd check it out."

"I see. Well, give my condolences to the widow. Anything else, Milt?"

"No. Thanks, Al, I really appreciate it."

"Don't mention it."

"Hey, I run a Laundromat—if you'd like, I'll press your next set of uniforms gratis."

"That's unnecessary but appreciated. Goodbye." The line goes dead, and Milt hangs up the phone.

"What's this really about, Jake?"

"Nothing good, Milt. Someone wants something and thinks Tony's widow has it. Right now I'm just trying to determine who the players are so I can identify a way out of this mess. But I know that I have to keep the cops at arm's length for the moment. It gives me an option to resolve my situation that disappears the moment they take over."

Milt stares at me like he can read my mind. "Okay. But if you change your mind..."

"Thanks, Milt—you'll be the first guy I call. If you hear anything, you can reach me at this number."

"New phone number in this day and age? With portability, I didn't think anybody ever changed their number. That is, unless their number isn't safe to use." His smile is tense.

2:00 p.m.
"Very personal and explicit..." Sarah

Back at the hotel, Sarah meets me in the lobby, and I catch her up on what I learned.

"Now it's your turn," I say to her once I finish.

"Sammy Bahn's been running a syndicate in Vegas for years. I talked to a cop buddy of mine in LA who said they were hearing rumors that Sammy was expanding up and down the West Coast. There have been lots of allegations of criminal activity, but I can't find that he's been indicted in the past five years. I obtained Tony's phone records from a friend of mine. I'm tracking down the owners of the numbers and hope to have a list of people he's been calling soon.

"Tony's partner is Phil Alberty. He's forty-two, graduated from U of O, never been married, and never been arrested. I haven't been able to find much on the partnership itself. "Last but not least is Heather. She wasn't truly last—I started with her." Sarah looks up from her notes at me.

"Go ahead—don't keep me in suspense."

"I couldn't find much of anything on the internet. But I pulled numbers she's dialed from her cell for the past year, plus I obtained her text messages. There's one number that keeps repeating. The owner is Gary Franklin. He owns a bar in Southeast." Sarah stops and looks at me yet again.

"And?"

"I'm not sure you want And."

"I do want And. Quit messing with me."

"They're a thing. The texts are very personal and explicit. She's been cheating on Tony for six months at least, all the way up to Tony's death."

I feel my blood racing. I'm angry. I want to hit my head against a wall. She wanted to be with me *and* Tony when we were kids. She gets married *and* cheats on her husband. How could I ever have expected her to change? No, that's not what hurts. What hurts is that she lied to me—just like she lied to me when we were kids. I feel the old anger, frustration, and jealously of that day at school come flooding back. It threatens to consume me. Back when I was the third wheel, I hurt every time I saw them touching and kissing. I know now why I enlisted in the army. I did it to save Tony's life, or at least my sanity, by locking myself away from them.

"Jake, listen to me."

I feel Sarah shaking me. I look at her.

"Jake, focus on me. Good—are you okay? I thought you were having a stroke or something. What gives?"

Sarah. What do I tell Sarah? "Everything," my little angel says. And so I do. I tell her about growing up. I tell her about Heather and me. I tell her about everything but the image of Heather standing in her room in a sliver of moonlight, dressed in a cotton nightgown.

"Just promise me one thing," Sarah says.

"What's that?"

"Don't reenlist."

I laugh a little. "No, I think I'm a bit more under control and wiser than back then."

"Well...at least you're older. Plus, they wouldn't take you."

"You know I'm hurting here, right? I thought you were going to be my comforting shoulder."

"As soon as we get the target off our backs, I'll be your camp counselor. But we need you to be focused. I don't think you want to let Heather know what we know."

"Why's that?"

"What if she's involved with Tony's death?" I begin to interrupt, but she silences me with her hand. "I know: no way, no how. But what if? We know they weren't happy. We know she was cheating on him. What if she wanted out of the marriage? Or what if Gary Franklin wanted Tony out of the way? It makes more sense than Sammy Bahn killing a guy who's got insurance."

"You're crazy. She may be a lying cheat, but she's not a killer."

"Fine, then it won't hurt to keep her in the dark until we prove who's responsible."

I think about going into the room and either confronting Heather or playacting. I don't think I can hide my pain and disappointment. "I can't go back up there, not tonight."

"I agree. I'll tell her you're tracking down some leads. I'll stay with her. Jake, don't hate her. She's just a person trying to find happiness and security. She didn't do any of this to hurt you. It's not personal, even if it feels like it is, and I get how it does. She's been an important part of your life. Don't burn bridges any sooner than you have to."

I look at Sarah and gather my thoughts. One minute Sarah seems ready to kick Heather to the curb, and the next she's telling me to not blame Heather for cheating on her husband. "You're not supposed to understand women," my little devil says. "They have a sensor telling them to flip directions when a man gets close to understanding them." My little angel makes a novel suggestion: "Why not tell her you're confused?" My little devil and I both tell him to shut up.

"I'm confused. Earlier I thought you were pretty angry at her for being with me. Why are you defending her?"

"Because I'm not emotionally invested and can see that you aren't capable of being rational around her right now. Take some time to think. Stay at my sister's—I'll let her know you're coming. One other thing, Jake: don't go looking for answers in a bottle."

I see the concern in her eyes. I begin to calm down, which isn't the same as feel good. It merely means I'm successfully suppressing my feelings until I get settled for the evening. "Okay, you're right. Call me, or Milt, if you need anything."

"I will." Sarah hugs me, then pushes away and walks to the elevator. As she boards, she smiles sadly at me and the doors close.

3:25 p.m.
"It was just physical..." Gary

I spend the next twenty minutes making sure I'm not being followed. Eventually, I make it to Southeast Portland. Even though I grew up here, I don't find myself in this part of town very often. When I do venture back into the old neighborhood, a wave of melancholy washes over me. It's funny how my mind chooses to remember the good times, at least at first. I think, *Why don't I spend more time over here?* But then I slowly remember the not so good times.

My little angel is tsk-tsking me. Even though I told Sarah I was headed to her sister's house, I can't help myself. I decide I should check out Heather's sex partner, Gary. Not the smartest thing to do, given my emotional investment, but I need to vent some excess energy.

The Sweet Tea Bar is located on Division Street. The exterior is strip-mall ugly in need of a rehab. Industrial-gray paint contrasts with the dirty old brick facade to form a dull backdrop to the store windows and signs. But inside, the bar is warm and comfortable. The tables and booths are positioned to allow for secluded conversation. The chairs and benches are stained wood with padded black leather seats. The floor is littered with peanut shells, and the bar itself is beautiful stained wood, fronting mirrors and rows of bottles. My favorite kind of place, one with lots of bottles. This time of day the place is about half-full. It's a Monday between meals, and the crowd looks comfortable and happy.

A female employee intent on obtaining my order comes by to check on me. I'm not quite sure what to call her; it used to be sweetheart, but I'm sure that if I say that, they'll do rude things to my food. Or it could be waitress, but not in front of Sarah, or it could be server, but that seems demeaning. How about food and beverage engineer?

"Hello, would you like a menu?"

"No, thanks. I just need a single malt scotch, one ice cube. Do you have Glenmorangie?"

"Yes, ten-, twelve-, or eighteen-year?"

"What the heck, let's try the eighteen. Make it a double." My little angel smacks me in the ribs. I tell him one drink isn't going to kill me.

"I'll be right back."

I know the drink is going to cost as much as I normally pay for a bottle, but I feel I deserve to lament my lame love life in luxury. There appears to be only one male working at the moment, and he's behind the bar. The server returns with my drink.

"Thanks. Say, I'm an investor in bars and restaurants. How do I contact the owner of this place? It seems to have a lot of charm."

"Gary's the owner, and he's behind the bar." She nods in his direction.

"That's great! Could you see if he has five minutes to talk to me?"

"I will." She smiles and walks to the bar. She speaks to Gary, who looks in my direction, smiles, and waves. He dries his hands on a towel and walks toward me.

"I'm the owner, Gary Franklin, Mr....?" Gary is a bit over six feet, in shape, with blond hair and bluish-gray eyes. My little devil wants to punch him because he's good-looking.

"Brand, Jake Brand. It's a pleasure to meet you. Do you have a few minutes to talk?"

"I'd be happy to. We're already staffed up for dinner, so I'm just in everyone's way. Hell, who am I kidding? They never really need me."

"Great. I really appreciate your taking the time."

"Sure. Cindy says you're an investor?"

"*I'm* not—I represent investors. They like small, unique, family-atmosphere places. This seems to fit the bill. You have a ring—are you married?"

"Ten years in December. I'm glad to hear you noticed the family vibe of this place. We were going for that—even though we've got a great bar. I've got two kids myself."

"Perfect. Family. The investors I represent don't take kindly to cheats and philanderers. Are you a philanderer?" My smile softens the bite of my forward question, but not entirely. Gary looks at me curiously. Something about me doesn't smell right.

"I'm not sure that's any of your business, Mr. Brand. But I'll tell you my wife and I are happy, and I take my wedding vows very seriously."

"Oh, I'm sure you do. Did your vows include a promise of fidelity?"

"Okay, that's enough. I don't know what kind of investors

you represent, but you're doing them a great disservice." Gary turns to leave.

"I lied. I'm a private investigator, and I'm investigating the death of Tony Weintraub. I think you're familiar with him, or at least his wife, aren't you?"

Gary's face turns crimson. He looks like he just finished his first day at spring break and forgot the sunscreen. "I don't like liars, Mr. Brand. What the hell do you want?"

"Since you're a cheater, I'm not sure I care what you do or don't like." I smile at him with no humor. "How about we both put posturing aside and I ask you a few questions. Then we both go on with our days as if this never happened."

"Fine. I had nothing to do with Tony's death. Are we done?"

"Not hardly. How long had you been sleeping with his wife?"

"That's none of your damned business."

"Probably not, but I could make it the business of the police. Which do you prefer, Gary, me or the police? Al Jenkins is the investigating officer. I could call him right now."

"Go ahead—I was here working when Tony was killed. And I have lots of witnesses. The police don't scare me at all."

"That may be true, but you still could have arranged for Tony to be killed. And then there's always your wife. Does she scare you?"

Gary's face moves from crimson to pale. "You're a bastard, aren't you?" Gary gulps down his pride and fury and sits back down. "Eight months. Okay? Heather and I saw each other for eight months. She came in here, had a couple of drinks, and told me her sad story. She and Tony weren't happy. One thing led to another. Jesus, I had nothing to do with Tony's death, Brand. Heather and I weren't, like, in love or anything. It was just physical. I had no reason to hurt Tony, none at all."

"Did Heather know it was just physical?"

"Absolutely—we talked about it. She's not a monogamous person, she says."

That's what I'm learning, no monogamy with Heather. All these years I thought she was just immature when she wanted both me and Tony. "What kinds of cars do you own?"

"Two Chevys. Why?"

"It's just a question." I look out the window at the parking lot—a painfully dull parking lot that does indeed contain a Chevy, three at least, and no Leafs. This isn't what I expected. I thought that I'd either beat the crap out of Gary or make him cry. Instead I'm the one who feels like crying.

5:06 p.m.
"All my friends call me Sammy..." Sammy

Sarah's sister, Carole, sets me up in a spare bedroom and lets me have private use of the back porch. I think she's concerned about the bottle I'm cracking open. My guess is Sarah gave her my résumé. I look up at the blue sky as the warm breeze brushes against my face. I pour myself two fingers and sip on my single malt scotch, savoring the burning sensation in my throat that bursts into flames in my belly. The smoky oak flavors mix with hints of orange that linger on my tongue.

Sarah is right. I can't condemn Heather. Just because she wants something different from me doesn't mean she's bad. It just means we're different. Sure, she cheated on Tony, but what right do I have to judge? I wasn't at their house observing their relationship. But she did lie to me. I'm having trouble understanding why she did that. What's the upside? Is it because she's involved in Tony's death? Maybe it's because she doesn't want to disappoint me. I want that to be the answer, but my little devil is screaming, "How do you spell *naïve*?" at the top of his lungs.

I light a cigarette and place it in an ashtray. I reposition the ashtray so that the smoke wafts across my face. In the old days I'd finish this bottle. Tonight it's one drink, and then I go to bed and pretend to sleep.

More and more I think Tony's death has nothing to do with Sammy. It could be anybody. Hell, it could be Sammy, but why would he kill Tony before he had secured the thumb drive?

I hear the doorbell ring. I hear Sarah's sister answer, and then the house goes quiet—too quiet. I get up and move to the open slider. I can see the family room and kitchen but not the front door. I can't hear anyone speaking, but I hear someone moving through the house to my right. And I think I hear someone else to my left. I wait outside, just around the corner next to the slider. Steps approach. Slowly a gun peeks through the doorway. I grab the wrists attached to the hands holding the gun and break their grip on the pistol. I grab it and point it at a man dressed in black. His eyes are big and surprised.

"Turn, face away, and lock your fingers behind your head," I whisper to him. He looks at me, searching for an opening where he can regain the gun. Seeing none, he slowly complies. I squeeze his interlaced fingers tightly with my left hand while holding the gun, pressed snuggly to his back, in my right.

"Tell your buddy to come visit us," I whisper.

"Found him," he yells.

Three people enter the room. One is Sarah's sister. A man is holding her arm. In his other hand is a gun pointed in my direction. The third person I recognize from his celebrity pictures. It's none other than Sammy "Knuckles" Bahn.

"Mr. Bahn, I'm a big fan of yours. It's a pleasure to make your acquaintance."

"That so? Well, I didn't know you from shit until recently. Why are you being so inhospitable to Benny there? He do you some harm?"

"Well, other than pointing a gun at me? No, he's been pretty quiet."

"Yeah, I bet. Tell you what. I'll send the girl to you; you send me Benny. He's my second-favorite nephew. You can even keep the gun. I know how some guys like insurance. We have a deal?"

I think about it for a minute and decide Sarah's sister is dead if I try anything. "Sure," I say. I release Benny, empty the gun of bullets, and hand it back to Benny.

"Nice touch, Mr. Brand. Maybe we can do some business. Benny, you and Jim go wait outside. I'll be okay. Ms., could you give Mr. Brand and me a few moments of privacy?"

Carole's speechless. I try smiling at her. I hope my face doesn't look like a fright mask. She just nods and heads down a hall toward a nervous breakdown.

"Mr. Bahn, join me for a scotch?"

"Love to. What a fucked-up couple of days."

I grab a glass from the kitchen, and we move outside to the deck and sit and sip the scotch.

"I see you smoke, Mr. Brand. I have some very fine cigars here. Would you like one?"

"Don't mind if I do."

Sammy is very relaxed. His face is young for a sixty-plus-year-old. His full head of gray hair is professionally styled. His gray eyes seem devoid of emotion in spite of a slight grin on his lips. He clips the ends of two cigars and hands one to me. We both light up, and I strategically place mine in the ashtray next to the remains of my cigarette.

"Mr. Brand, I'm concerned that you may have come into possession of property that belongs to me. And I'm hoping you're a reasonable man. I'd like the property back, and we all go on living our happy, productive lives."

"I'd like nothing more than to work with you, Mr. Bahn. But I need to know something first."

"Shoot."

"Who killed Tony?"

Sammy takes a long drag on his cigar and examines the fiery tip. He moves his fingers so the cigar turns as he phrases his response.

"Mr. Brand, about thirty years ago, my dad, whom I loved dearly, caught a chump stealing. My dad had the chump beat to death. The cops put two and two together and came up with fifteen to twenty for my dad. He died in prison. I learned a very valuable lesson that day. If a guy does you wrong, don't punish him and get caught. Especially when that guy is holding documents that might be embarrassing. So, to answer your unspoken question, it wasn't me. I don't hurt people no more. These days, I use intellectual reason. Sometimes I just make sure their enemies or the cops find incriminating evidence against them. No reason to dirty my hands...if it can be avoided. Plus, if you have the property, you know I couldn't kill him. I was too exposed. My nephew Benny's been running the franchise here in Portland, and he says he has no idea who took Tony down."

"That's kind of what I was figuring. I was hoping I could give you your property, and we could just pretend none of this happened."

"Mr. Brand, you know how the brain works. It remembers everything; it's part of self-preservation. No, I don't think we forget. I think we remember this fine cigar and beautiful scotch and the fact that we are both reasonable men."

"I'd like that, Mr. Bahn."

"Call me Sammy. All my friends call me Sammy."

6:20 p.m.
"You don't have leverage..." Sammy

I try to figure Sammy out. I need allies, but can I trust him? If I give Sammy the drive, he's out of the picture. And I can't go to the cops with the drive without them looking at Sammy. I need to convince him to join forces with me or I'm going to be involved in a shoot-out, either with the guys who killed Tony or with Sammy. "I think you should care about who killed Tony."

Sammy looks at me while wisps of smoke flow out of his mouth. "Why's that, Jake?"

"What if Tony's death wasn't an accident and was intended to flush your property out into the open? Could be someone's using the cops and Tony's insurance against you."

"Funny you should mention that, Jake—I was thinking the same thing. I was, really. But the way I figure, I secure my property, head back to Vegas, and there's nothin' they can do. I'm golden again."

"Except they won't stop there; would you? They've killed a man. They've proven they don't have limits. Think about it. They obviously want something badly. I don't think they'll stop until you're a speed bump, just like Tony. Hell, their next step could be to tip off the police about Brown Construction. Get the police to start digging around the architecture firm. It won't take them long to put you on top of Tony's death dance card."

Sammy ponders my comments for a few minutes. "Okay, let's say you're right. I ain't a cop. The real cops haven't been able to find Tony's killer. You're the big-boy detective. What can I do that you and they can't? And why should I believe that you care about what happens to me?"

"I care because, if I'm right, these guys will continue to put pressure on Tony's widow, Heather. She won't be safe if they think she still has the property. If you're not in jail, they'll think she's still holding the ball. I can't let that happen. I'm more than happy to be the point man on this project. But you need to help me. I need information on who's been tailing me since Tony's funeral. If it wasn't you, then I need to figure out who it was. And I need eyes on the street. I can't ask the police to look around for me. Maybe you can, but I don't want the police to begin asking the wrong questions. I think you know what I mean." I watch as he lets my comments settle. I've tried to make sure I'm not threatening him—I'm warning him. But he has to know that if we don't get rid of the bad guys I will continue to be a threat.

"Unfortunately, Jake, I do. What do you suggest?"

"First, let's get your property. I want to get it out of our possession as fast as possible. Second, you check with your guys. Someone put a tracer on my Jeep at the funeral or shortly after. I want to know who. Third, the police never recovered the Nissan Leaf that hit Tony. It's beat-up and isn't being repaired at any public location. I was thinking it might be buried somewhere, or maybe it went to a chop shop. You could check your connections for that."

"All of that is fine with me. Just remember, no matter what happens, you don't have leverage with what you know. You have a liability. Look at me, Jake. Your health and the well-being of your friends depend on my being able to trust you. Am I clear?"

"Crystal."

He looks back to the glow of his cigar.

"I need to know how you found me."

He smiles and says, "Benny did some background checks on you and your assistant. Discovered she had a sister in town and had a couple of the boys sit on the place. When you showed, they called us, and here we are."

He studies me like a poker player reading a chump who's gone all in. "Okay, let's go get my property. You mind telling me where we're headed?"

"The Phoenix Inn in Lake Oswego."

"Good, we'll follow you."

I call Sarah and let her know that we're coming. We should be there in twenty minutes. She says that sounds fine to her; she'd just as soon get rid of the drive as quickly as possible.

6:50 p.m.
"It won't do any good to run..." Jake

Sammy and I park, enter the motel, and take the elevator up to the fourth floor. I knock on the door. "It's me."

The door opens, and Sarah is standing with her gun drawn but pointed down. "Jake, Mr. Bahn."

"Sammy, this is Sarah."

"Jake, you didn't tell me you had such a lovely assistant." Sammy takes Sarah's hand in both of his and kisses it. Sarah looks at him like he's a grandpa with halitosis.

"Not in the hallway," I say. Sammy and I enter the room, and I introduce him to Heather. Sarah is nervous, and Heather clearly doesn't know what to think. "Sammy didn't kill Tony. I've made a deal with him: he gets the thumb drive, and we get to be friends."

A burst of police sirens interrupts the pleasantries, and then Sammy's phone rings. He pulls it out of his jacket and answers. "Yeah. Okay." He hangs up and looks at us. "Somehow the cops figured out we're here. They're outside, taking down my boys. I hope none of you had a wagging tongue."

"Last thing we want, Sammy, is to be caught with you and the drive. There's no future in that play."

He shakes his head. "Where's the back exit?"

"It won't do any good to run, Sammy. If they know we're here and they catch us running, things only get worse. Plus, how long do you think even you can run from the cops in this day and age? No, we need to be the innocent types."

"But the thumb drive will burn me."

"Don't worry about the thumb drive. I've taken care of that," Sarah says.

Sammy and I look at her, wondering what she can possibly mean. But we don't have time to ask. We hear a knock on the door. "Police! Open up."

"No one talks to them. Ask for an attorney and don't say a word until you get one," I tell them. They all nod. "Sarah, we need to get our guns on the bed so they don't shoot us. They might hesitate to shoot you, but they'd probably fight over who gets to shoot me." We unload our guns and place them on one of the beds. Sarah joins the others at the far side of the room as I open the door. Three police officers move in, guns drawn. "We have a warrant to search this room and your persons. Sir, please step over toward the back wall with the rest of the folks. These officers will be searching the premises as I interview and search each of you. Who is the owner of the guns on the bed?"

"Her and me—we both have permits in our wallets."

"Okay, then let's start with you. Please come out into the hallway with me." The officer and I exit the room and a fourth officer moves in to watch Sammy, Heather, and Sarah while the other two sweep the room. The commotion has brought unwanted attention from several temporary residents of the floor. If this were a freeway, the rubberneckers would have the traffic at a standstill. The officer sees them as well. "All right, everyone please go back to your rooms and keep your doors closed and locked. Nothing to see here."

One lady is staring hard at me. I can tell by her "shame on you" face that she'd vote to hang without a trial. I stick my tongue out at her. Her face registers shock and then disgust as she slams her door behind her.

"You always this mature?"

"Rarely. I usually act like a child. Officer, may I ask what you're searching for?" I pull out my wallet and hand him my driver's license and handgun permit.

"Drugs. We received an anonymous tip that there was a drug deal going down here, Mr. Brand." He reads my ID and hands it back to me. "What is the purpose of this meeting?"

"I don't think I have to tell you that."

"You will if we find any drugs or evidence of illegal activity." The cop smiles and nudges my shoulder. "Probably not drugs, right? Those young ladies look pretty eager. Be honest—you and your dad are buying a little companionship?"

I move closer to the cop and softly say to him, "Officer, if you say that out loud in front of those 'young ladies,' there's a 100 percent chance you'll be locking one of them up for assaulting an officer. Well, that's not entirely true. Your buddies will be locking her up. You'll be in the hospital." I step back and smile at him.

I can see that I've had an effect on him. He turns slightly toward the room while continuing to stare at me. "Connor, cuff them. We'll have our conversation down at the station." He turns his full attention to me. "Assume the position, ass-wipe.

7:30 p.m.
"And two detectives enter..." Jake

The ride to the jail is quiet. I'm in the backseat with Sarah. Sammy and Heather are in one of the other cars. We've been told not to speak. The cop in front isn't particularly interested in us—it's just another night of hauling handcuffed humans to cages. The only sounds come from his radio, and I'm all out of interest for the police-band chatter.

The car stinks. I can tell by Sarah's facial expression that she is much more aware of the odor than I am. Her nose is like a bloodhound's. She can tell if I've been near a cigarette from twenty feet away. She can even determine whether it was from a recent car ride or a visit to a bar. Apparently they have different textures.

We arrive at the jail, and the cops split us up. I'm not sure where they're taking the others, but I'm taken to my own private interrogation room to stew and soften. The fear of the unknown is supposed to turn me to mush. I'm not afraid of being arrested. But I am afraid of what happens when the cops start asking about the information on the confiscated laptop and thumb drive. All of a sudden, Sarah, Heather, and I are witnesses as to the authenticity of the information on the drive. And the information on that drive could be a nail in Sammy's coffin. Of course, that assumes that Sammy allows us to live long enough to testify.

The room is just like they look on TV. There's one door and a large mirror through which I'm certain they're watching me. I know they're recording everything that happens in the room. The walls, floor, ceiling, and furniture are all gray. I decide to take a nap, or at least appear to do so. I fold my hands in my lap and close my eyes. I take several long breaths to clear my mind and let my head rest on my chest. Meditation and exercise—I know about both, but I've been choosing drink and smokes.

The door to my suite opens, and two detectives enter. One leans against a wall and stares at me. "He must be the bad cop," my little devil says. The second reads through a file as he nonchalantly sits at the table across from me. Finally he looks up at me and smiles. "Smoke?"

"Sure."

He lights a cigarette, hands it to me, and pushes a coffee mug toward me.

"I thought we weren't allowed to smoke in public buildings. Are you going to charge me for this violation?"

The detective smiles as he lights a second cigarette and begins to puff away. "I won't tell if you don't."

"When do I get to call my lawyer?"

"You can call him now. But if you do, we'll take you back to a cell. You and your friends will sit there for twelve hours while we try to remember where we left you. Then maybe for another twenty-four hours we lose your file. You see how disorganized we can be? It's a shame. Or you can answer a couple of questions and be on your way—your choice."

"What are the charges against us?"

"Right now there aren't any charges."

"Then I'd like to leave."

"I'm sure you would. But unfortunately, you are a material witness to a crime. For your own safety, we will hold you until you've answered a few questions."

"And what might that crime be?"

The cop leans back in his chair while looking at me. He turns his head toward the bad cop but never takes his eyes off of me. "Solicitation, wasn't that what Officer Pelen said?"

The bad cop smiles and replies, "Solicitation, smuggling, jay walking, illegal parking..."

The not-so-bad cop turns back to me. "Wow, that sounds like we have a lot to investigate; could take a while. Come on, Jake, you know that we can keep you here longer than you can pretend to sleep. Just answer a few questions."

"Well, against my better judgment, I'll at least listen."

"Good. Why were you at the hotel?"

"I can't disclose that."

"Aw, client work. You know that a private detective doesn't have attorney-client privilege, right?"

"I know, but I still can't disclose any information about my client unless I'm legally forced to or he or she gives me permission. And since you obviously don't have any probable cause, you're not going to get a subpoena to force me. Am I close?"

"Well, sort of. Right now our tech guy is going through the computer and the thumb drive. What do you think he's going to find, Jake?"

"I don't know. And even if I did, I couldn't disclose that information."

"I see. You know, it isn't often that we get celebrity criminals in Lake Oswego. Sammy Bahn has quite the rep. I imagine he has all kinds of baggage. I imagine he always has baggage *on him*. If he does right now, you're an accomplice. Who knows, maybe he has a murder weapon, or drugs, or something that ties him to a long stay in prison. I'll bet you could even be his cellmate."

The door opens, and another detective enters and hands my desk mate a new file. He begins to read the contents. He laughs and sets it down.

"Want to know what's in the file?"

"No."

I try to control my demeanor as adrenaline fires through my body. It makes me want to jump up and run out of here screaming like a madman. Instead I lean over my cigarette and take a big whiff. I turn toward the detective and smile back. "And?"

He looks at me, looks at his buddies, and they all leave.

I try to project calm, but I'm churning. I really wanted him to respond to my And. I think about Sarah, confined somewhere and feeling vulnerable. I think about Sammy, smiling at some cop and telling stories about how his dad used to own tougher cops. But mostly I think about Heather. I think about how much I want her in my life. But I can't make sense of her. She never seems happy with just one man. And I still don't understand why she lied to me. I know the adult thing to do would be to talk to her about it. The Jake way would be to enlist in the army. Well, that's out. Sarah's right—I'm too old.

After about thirty minutes, the door opens, and one of the detectives enters. "You're free to go. Follow this officer to collect your belongings." Just as I'm about to exit the room, he says, "Mr. Brand."

I turn and look at him. On TV this is where the loaded question hits you square between the eyes. "Yes?"

"Don't you want to take your cigarette?"

"No, thanks, those things will kill you."

11:20 p.m.
"Scotch, anyone?" Sammy

Outside of the police station, I see Sammy's muscle. I walk over to them. "Is Sammy out?"

"No, you're the first."

"Okay. Do you have a lawyer on the way?"

"He's in there; been there almost as long as you. They told us this was a drug bust. Sammy don't never deal in drugs."

"Yeah, that was just an excuse so the cops could bring us in. But they don't have anything."

"Hey, ain't that your friends?"

I turn back toward the police station in time to see Sarah and then Heather walk out. They see me and head in our direction. As they reach us, Sammy exits the station along with a GQ-clothed man. Probably his attorney. They shaked hands and join us in the parking lot.

As they arrive, I am giving both Sarah and Heather big hugs. Sammy looks at me with a "don't even think about it" stare.

"Well, Mr. Brand, seems you're right. Someone wants me. Someone called in an anonymous tip that we were dealing in drugs. But I think it's pretty clear they were after the thumb drive."

"Not here. Let's go someplace quiet," I say

"I'm renting a place not too far away. Boys, I'll drive this group to the house. You get a cab and catch up."

Sarah looks questioningly at me. Maybe she's remembering the rule about not riding with strangers, or the one about not riding with known mob bosses or suspected killers. I shrug and get into the car. If Sammy wants to whack us, he won't do it himself, and he won't do it in his car.

With the four of us in his Mercedes sedan, Sammy drives us to the actual lake in Lake Oswego. His rented home is spacious and elegant. The back opens up to a large deck that overlooks a sloping yard, down to an extensive garden and the lake Oswego itself. Lights twinkle all along its shore. They seem magical, fairylike. "You've been reading too much Peter Pan," my little devil says.

"Scotch, anyone?"

We all say yes. With drink in hand, and a bottle on the table, Sammy lights a cigar, as do Heather and I. Sarah shifts her chair to be upwind of the three of us. I can see her looking nervously at my drink.

"Just one, Sarah, no worries," I whisper to her.

"Okay, Mr. Detective, what just happened?" Sammy asks.

"Like I told you earlier, someone wants to take you down. They used a bogus drug deal tip to get the police to harass us. The police were supposed to find the thumb drive, which leads me to my first question." I turn toward Sarah. "Want to explain how we aren't charged with several felonies?"

"Just to be safe, I bought an identical thumb drive and laptop. I stored the actual stuff in a laundry closet after you called to let me know you and Sammy were on your way. No disrespect intended, Mr. Bahn..."

"Sammy."

"Sammy. But I just thought it might be nice to have a backup plan. I had used the hidden laptop to do my work and had given the duplicate to Heather. I told her to load stuff on the drive and do innocuous internet searches."

Heather smiles. "The thumb drive has several hundred recipes. I like to cook, so I just searched for interesting recipes and loaded as many as I could."

Sammy laughs. "Sarah, you interested in a new career? I could use you on my security team."

She smiles at Sammy and then at me. "Nah, I have to keep this big lug out of jail. He thinks life is a game of Monopoly and I'm his "get out of jail free" card."

I feel a wave of relief wash over me. Even though I don't think Sarah would ever take Sammy up on his offer, I can't help but have a twinge of angst. What would life be like without Sarah? I don't like that thought at all.

"Jake, it seems that you were right. I'm still a target; Tony was a lever." He hesitates, looks at Heather. We all do. I see pain in her eyes, just before she looks away and sniffles. "That was very indelicate of me, Heather. Please accept my apology. It has to be awfully painful to know that Tony was killed for any reason, let alone something like this."

"Thank you, Sammy. Umm, where is the restroom?" A full stream of tears is right on the edge now.

Sammy instructs her, and she leaves.

"So, you want me to see if I can find the Nissan Leaf. What else?"

"Someone tracked us to the motel. You should check your car for a tracer. If there isn't one, then either they followed you to Carole's house and from there to the motel or one of your guys is working against you."

"Why don't you check my car for the tracer right now? Tell my boys I need them in here. If my car is clean, we'll consider next steps."

I can tell by the look in his eyes that Heather, Sarah, and I don't want to be around for next steps. I walk back outside and tell the muscle that Sammy wants them inside. Once they're out of sight, I begin searching the car. Bingo, I find the tracer in the rear wheel well on the driver's side.

I go back inside, and Sammy sends his boys away. "Well?"

"There's a tracer."

"Let me see it."

"I left it, for now. We may be able to use it to our advantage."

Heather glances at me and then wanders down to the garden. I stand, excuse myself, and walk toward her. Out of the corner of my eye, I see Sarah staring at the pavers.

When I reach Heather, she is standing in the moonlight. We are shielded from the patio by masterfully maintained bushes and small trees. The lake is in front of us. Its surface is still but for an occasional wake washing in from a slow-moving boat lit with running lights. I stand next to her, and she wraps her arms around me. I put my right arm around her.

"What's wrong? I feel you shutting down on me again." She sighs.

I pause before I respond. My little angel tells me honesty is the best policy. My little devil says I should kiss her and forget about the lie. "Sarah checked you out. She thinks you've been having an affair. You told me you weren't." I don't tell her I've already confirmed the story. I want to see where she goes with the unstated question.

I feel her tense and then hear her begin to cry. "Tony and I had been unhappy for a couple of years. I was lonely. You know me, Jake; I need a man like I need oxygen. Without one I would suffocate and die."

"But why lie to me? What did you gain by lying to me?"

"It was a stupid thing to do. I just...I just..."

I wait for her to gather her thoughts. In spite of my hurt, her presence is soothing and comfortable. And that thought frightens me. Even though we were best friends for a lot of years, I barely know this woman. My feelings for her are based upon a bunch of memories. It's as if we've been together all of these years, teenage Heather and me. I realize that I'm more wrapped up in Heather and our shared past than my divorce. I don't know if that's the healthy side of moving on or a testament to how much impact Heather has had on me.

"Jake, I didn't want to hurt you. After we, well...I just remember the way you reacted when we were kids, the way you closed down. You stopped being a friend. I didn't want to lose your friendship again. It means so much to me."

I look down at her and see desperation in her eyes. I see a plea for me to do something. I lean over, and we kiss. For some reason this kiss is different. It isn't a rushed and wild kiss between two kids. And it isn't a kiss between two recently united old friends. It's a kiss between two people in search of happiness and finding comfort for a moment in each other's arms.

She pulls away and smiles at me. "Jake, I want to be with you. I want to find out who we are as a couple. I know I've lied, and I know I hurt you when we were kids."

I begin to respond, and she places her index finger on my lips. "Don't say anything. Think about it. If you want me, I'm here, I'm yours. If you don't, I understand." She smiles and kisses me again. Then turns and walks back to the others.

Tuesday, July 26

8:00 a.m.

"Oh my, oh my, oh my..." Phil

Sammy insists that we spend the night. His insistent invitation has the flavor of an order, as if we're hostages until he has the drive in his hand. We all agree it probably doesn't make sense to head back to the motel tonight, so we all agree to accept his offer. His house is so big I feel like I have a wing all to myself. As much as I wanted to be with Heather, it felt uncomfortable around Sarah. So I'm on my own. My room is on the second floor facing the west, with a view of the lake.

In the morning I watch the sunrise slowly color the trees around the lake. It begins at the tips and works its way down to the water. I shower and head downstairs, where I find Sammy at a dining room table, drinking coffee and flipping through a newspapers.

"Good morning, Sammy."

"Good morning, Jake. Come join me for some breakfast."

"A cup of coffee and a piece of toast would be great. Then I've got to take off. Have you seen the ladies yet?"

"Sarah left about twenty minutes ago to get the drive." As I start to protest that it isn't safe, Sammy holds up a hand to silence me. "I know what you're going to say. She'll be fine. I have a couple of guys keeping an eye on her from a distance. Though, to be quite frank, I think she's tougher than the two of them combined."

I smile at that, pour myself some coffee, and grab a piece of toast. "Sammy, I don't know about you, but I'm tired of reacting. I'm going to start asserting some pressure of my own."

"Oh, I like the sound of that. Want company?"

"No, I'd better do this by myself. I plan on getting my Jeep back. Then I'm going to pay Tony's partner a call. He's my best guess as the guy behind all of this at the moment."

"I thought about him," Sammy says. "But I don't think he has the balls for this kind of action. He likes safe cash. He's not a tough guy. But you gotta start somewhere. I'll have info on the chop shops this morning. I have a buddy who can find out what's what quickly and quietly. I'll give you a call the moment I learn anything."

"Thanks, Sammy. You'll keep an eye on Heather and Sarah?"

"Of course, you are all welcome to stay here as long as necessary."

"Let the ladies know I'll be in touch soon."

My cab arrives and takes me to the car rental store, where I pick up my Jeep. I've decided that if someone is after us, I want them to target me. If I'm out in the open, maybe I can draw them away from Heather. I check to make sure there isn't a tracer or a booby trap of some sort, and drive away.

An hour later I park in a multistory parking structure in downtown Portland. Tony's architecture firm is in a twenty-story building on Third Avenue. I ride an elevator up to the eighteenth floor and exit into the lobby of Alberty and Weintraub, LLC.

The lobby is spacious, with a view of the south side of Portland, including the Willamette River. A friendly-looking receptionist smiles at me and asks if she can be of assistance. I introduce myself as a financial planner representing Heather and looking for Mr. Alberty. Ten minutes later a hulk of a man comes out and greets me.

"I'm Phil Alberty, Mr. Brand. Please come into my office."

I follow Phil, a six-feet-four flabby guy with thinning gray hair and perfectly pressed clothes. His office is roomy, with an executive desk as well as a small conference table. Phil moves around the desk and invites me to sit.

"So, hmm, Mr. Brand, neither Heather nor Tony ever mentioned you before. How long have you been working with them?"

"Not long, but I've known them since they were kids."

Phil's brain starts to churn, and I can almost see his cranium bulging. "Hmm, that's interesting. I remember Tony talking about you a couple of times. But I don't remember you being in finance."

"I'm not, directly. I'm more of a private investigator, bodyguard, and attack-dog kind of financial guy."

Phil's chugging brain advances from confused to defensive. "Mr. Brand, I'm afraid you'll need to leave. Hmm, you aren't who you represented yourself to be—"

"Of course, I can leave. I'll just let Sammy know that you weren't forthcoming. That was his word, *forthcoming*. I'm sure he'll be happy to discuss the situation directly with you." I stand and extend my hand. "Phil, it's been good to know you."

Phil's face moves two shades toward gray as he asks, "Mr. Bahn? What does he have to do with you?"

"Are you really going to play stupid? Okay, for a minute I can be patient. As we both know, Sammy, via Brown Construction, is your special client. Sammy knows about the skimming, and he's not happy. But he's mostly displeased about Tony. So, are you still stupid, or are you ready to chat?"

"Skimming? I—"

"Had better shut up. That's what you were about to say. Invite me to sit again so we can finish the conversation. Go ahead, ask me."

Phil stares at me questioningly, wondering if I'm serious about the invitation to sit. Seeing that I'm not making my way to a chair, he breaks down. "Please sit, Mr. Brand. Maybe I should be more patient, hmm. I certainly wouldn't want to inconvenience Mr. Bahn." I see beads of sweat forming on his forehead. Pretty soon he'll have dark half moons in the armpits of his suit coat.

"That's funny—that's exactly what Sammy said, *inconvenience*. He said it right after he told me you killed Tony. I said, 'Really? Let's go to the police.' Then Sammy said, 'No, Jake, the police would *inconvenience* me. Why doesn't Benny pay Phil a visit?' Have you met Benny? Yes? Well, you know he's not much of a conversationalist. Anyway, I said, 'No, Sammy, how about I meet with Phil. I'm sure he'll want to cooperate.' Sammy was pretty skeptical, but he said, 'What the hell. Give Phil an opportunity.' So, Phil, that's what this visit is about. It's your opportunity to get right with Sammy. It's your call: me, Benny, or the police?" I pause and smile at Phil as he goes from gray to downright ashen. "Take your time. I've got a few minutes to burn before my next meeting." I look at my watch and then out his window while his half moons grow to three-quarters.

"Oh my, oh my, oh my. No, please, Mr. Brand. Hmm, I had nothing to do with Tony's death. I swear. I was just as shocked as anyone. Tony and I were partners and friends. Why would I kill him?"

"Money is my guess. Sammy thinks you're just stupid. But I think it's all about the dinero."

"Jake—"

"Mr. Brand."

"Hmm, sorry, Mr. Brand, you must believe me. There's more money running through this place than I could spend in three lifetimes. Hmm, no, no, no, I had nothing to gain from Tony's death. Quite the opposite is true. Killing Tony just agitates the police. The last thing I want is the police nosing around here."

"Right, the fraud; did you know that Tony had insurance?"

Phil goes from ashen to scarlet. "Well…"

"Opportunity is walking away, Phil. Hear her footsteps? I think she's wearing heels. Better answer my questions quickly and honestly. Hesitation leads to skepticism."

"Yes, yes, yes, I did. I, I told him not to do it, but he didn't trust anyone. I don't know if you know, but he had started doing drugs and was becoming more and more paranoid. Hmm, he told me that he thought someone was following him, checking him out. I thought it was the drugs. I never for a moment thought he was in trouble. Please, Mr. Brand."

"Did you tell the police?"

"No, no, no, that would have led to too many uncomfortable questions. Hmm, no, no, no, keep the police away. Sammy can't want that."

"Did Tony ever say anything about who was following him?"

"He said it might be someone from the city. But that was it."

"When did he—" My phone rings, and I hold a hand up to Phil as I answer it. "Excuse me, Phil, I need some privacy. Can you wait outside?"

"Hmm, sure, I'll be right outside the door."

My little devil laughs as I kick Phil out of his own office. I answer the phone as Phil closes the door. "Yes?"

"You know who this is?" I recognize Sammy's voice.

"Yes."

"I found the chop shop. They fixed the Nissan. It was delivered and picked up by the same guy. Of course there wasn't any paperwork. The job was paid for in cash. They describe the guy as white, just over six feet, with gray, thinning hair, and a little paunchy. But there was a little bit of good news. This place likes to track info just in case something happens. They wrote down the VIN. I traced it and found the owner."

"Who is it?"

"Turns out the car is owned by the City of Portland. It's part of the motor pool.

9:52 a.m.
"Are you negotiating, Phil..." Jake

I call Phil back into his office. His time in the hall wasn't therapeutic. He's just as crimson as he was when he left the office. "That was Sammy. He's getting anxious and wants answers now. I told him what you've told me, and he says it isn't enough. He says either you killed Tony or you're purposely holding back. Phil, even if you didn't kill Tony, you're at risk. Sammy's telling me you're expendable." His face goes from crimson to pallid. My little devil is giving my angel 5:2 odds that pretty soon I'll be giving Phil CPR. My little angel is giving my devil 5:2 odds that I'll let him die before I give him CPR.

Phil collapses into a chair and lays his head in his hands. He's beginning to mutter and moan. He's losing it fast. I put my hand on his shoulder, and he jumps like I threw a punch at him. "Easy, big guy, I'm not going to hurt you. It's Sammy who isn't so cultured."

"Jesus, Mr. Brand, I don't know anything. No, no, no, I swear to God I don't. Hmm, I'll do anything to prove it. Anything—just tell me what I can do."

"I was hoping you'd feel that way. You need to deliver some information ASAP. And you need to be careful—if Tony's killer discovers you're looking for him, you'll be a target. Though if you don't help, you'll be on Sammy's list."

"Anything, please, please, please, just tell me what it is."

"Okay, you say that Tony thought it was someone from the city. Who at the city did Tony interact with? What departments should we be looking at?"

"Well, mostly city planning, hmm. We'd meet with the city manager, the city council, and occasionally the mayor. That's about it."

"This is what I need. First, you're going to get a physical description of every male in those departments. If you think of another department that you interact with, add it to the list. Second, you're going to get me access to all of the city's databases. And I mean all of them. And I need it all immediately."

Phil throws me off balance by smiling for the first time since he realized who I was. "That's next to impossible, and you know it. But if I can get all of that, you'll keep Sammy happy?"

"Are you negotiating, Phil? I don't see any good cards on the table in front of you, and you're all in. And I mean *all* in."

"No, not negotiating. No, I just want to know that you'll tell Sammy I did the impossible. That is, if I can get it done."

"He's trapping you, Jake. He's got cards up his sleeve," my little angel says. "Call his bluff, look at his cards, and take all the chips. He can't stop you," my little devil replies. "Sure, I'll tell Sammy you were a stand-up guy," *for whatever that's worth*, I finish silently.

He stands and walks to his computer. "Hmm, what's your email address?" I give it to him. "I'm sending you an email with an attachment. The attachment includes log-in info and passwords for all of the city's databases. One of them is personnel. They keep pictures that are used for security passes."

"How did you get the passwords?"

"Hmm, over time Tony and I realized that inside info was gold to us. So we bribed, tricked, whatever. Benny did most of the work—we just gave him a list of names. But it's not just passwords—it's key codes that the city's programmers use to get in to the city system. I don't think the city knows these exist. Our IT guy says no way do they know."

I smile at Phil. He's just bought himself a couple of days, maybe even years.

10:25 a.m.
"I have names and departments..." Sarah

Sarah and I meet at my condo. It's in the Pearl District of Northwest Portland. The contemporary space is composed of wide-plank hardwood floors and twenty-foot ceilings with exposed heat ducting and crisscrossing pipes. Warm whites, grays, and blues soften the harshness of the metal and glass. Along the west side, I have an unobstructed view of the West Hills and the north end of downtown. During the day my eyes feast on green firs. At night the lights of the city sparkle and wink at me. But it's lost some of its luster since Sue moved out. Sarah's presence helps me to push my memories of Sue aside temporarily, as that space in my brain fills with old and new memories of Heather.

We review where we are in the case and what the next steps are. Sarah worries that being out in the open like this makes us vulnerable, but we can't hide forever. Sometimes the only way to end a standoff is to stand up. Hopefully, I don't stand up into the crosshairs of a gun.

"Let's go to the motor pool page first," I tell Sarah. I've given her a rundown on my meeting with Phil.

"Here's the password, user name, and a link. This is pretty slick—they have it set up to automatically log on from this Excel spreadsheet." Sarah clicks on a link. "I assume you want me to find out who used the Nissan the night of Tony's death."

"That's right."

Sarah pecks at her keyboard for a minute. "Here's a list, but it doesn't identify the cars by VIN here. I'll bet that's on the insurance policies, though. But each car does have a unit number. On the night of Tony's death, there were five being used. Three of those were being used by males. What next?"

"Can you tell when they were returned? Ours would have been returned three-plus days after Tony was hit because of the repair work."

"Two meet that time frame. I have names and departments."

"Okay, let's go to personnel."

Her fingernails sound like tiny firecrackers as they tap the keys in rapid succession.

"Personnel: first guy is black; second guy is white. Ari Witten: white guy, six feet two, and weighs two sixty. He has thinning gray hair. I think this could be the guy who was watching you at the Hall Street Grill the other night. His hair is a little longer in the picture. What next?"

"I apply pressure to see if he breaks. If that doesn't work, we introduce him to Sammy. When does he work?"

Sarah hits a few keys and finds Witten's work schedule. "He's off today."

"Okay, get me his home address. I'll go there right now. Why don't you head over to Sammy's and check on Heather?"

I take off in my Jeep—no hiding now. I want this guy to come at me. Ari Witten has worked for the city just shy of a year. He lives in Tualatin, a burb south of Portland. It takes me twenty minutes to get there.

11:45 a.m.
"A figure of speech..." Jake

No one answers Ari's front door, so I casually wander around the side of the house to the backyard. The house is painted beige with white trim. It's a one-story ranch probably built in the '70s. I look into windows but don't see any dead bodies or mounds of cash waiting to be discovered. I see a set of dog dishes and become nervous about the prospect of being licked into submission. All of the doors and windows are locked, and I can see an alarm pad inside the back door. I have a feeling that something's not right. I decide that the feeling is my little angel telling me it's probably too early in the game to be breaking into Ari's house. It's okay when you know a guy is a killer. When you just think he's a killer, you have to act with more restraint. Plus, I don't want to tip him off that I'm watching him until I can confront him and watch his reaction.

As I'm about to walk back to my car, a flash of red and white at ground level, at the back of the yard, catches my eye. The color looks out of place in and among the greens and browns. But a ray of sunlight has spotlighted it for the moment. I turn and examine the unkempt, fenced garden. I walk back, and decide that the color is a cloth of some sort. It's probably nothing, but I'm here, might as well be thorough. When I'm a few feet away, I see that the cloth is red with fresh blood. I pull my gun and take another quick look around the yard for threats. Seeing none, I move closer to the cloth. I kneel and pull at a corner of the cloth that hasn't been soaked with blood. Underneath is a beagle with a freshly cut throat. "Sorry, Bowser, bad luck can happen to any of us." I gently replace cloth over the dog, and I move back to the house. "Anyone who would kill a dog deserves some pain," my little angel says.

I decide stealth isn't a concern anymore. I walk back to the house and kick the door twice. It bursts open. The security alarm remains silent like it's not even set. I move into the house, entering the kitchen and dining area. On the kitchen floor is Ari, a single bullet wound in between his eyes. The skin around the wound is scorched—he was shot up close. His wide eyes stare at the popcorn ceiling. I can't imagine that ugly ceiling being the last thing I see. I reach down and touch his neck; it's still warm, he hasn't been dead long. I move quickly and quietly through the house but find no one hiding. I look closer at the body but don't see anything of interest.

I have confirmation that Ari is in the middle of it, but I don't have him to beat into a confession. "It's kind of sad, don't you think?" my little angel asks. "Oh please, who cares about this punk?" my little devil asks. "Not him, moron—Bowser!" My little angel replies. "Oh, right," my little devil sadly agrees.

I decide there's nothing more to gain here, and I don't want to be caught with a murder victim. I walk as casually as I can to my Jeep. I drive until I can find a convenience store. I buy a burner and call 911. I try to disguise my voice as best as possible. "Don't interrupt—I'm only going to say this once. There's a dead man and dog at..." I give them the address, destroy the phone, and toss it in the trash.

On my way back to the office, I try to think who would kill Ari. Clearly he was involved in Tony's death, and Ari's partner or partners decided to tie up a loose end. I could tell by the condition of the blood on the floor and the heat of his body that he hadn't been dead long. I couldn't have missed the killer by more than thirty minutes. And somebody knew I was on to him. As far as I know, only Sarah knows about Ari. Phil had no idea who we were after. At the time I met with him, I didn't know about Ari. The only other person with any information was Sammy. Sammy knew about the city car and had a description of the driver. But why would he share info with me and then turn around and kill Ari? No, Sammy wasn't behind this. Or maybe not Sammy—maybe one of Sammy's boys? They knew we were at the Phoenix Inn, and they would have known that we were close to identifying Ari when Sammy found the chop shop. That made the most sense.

I park and walk up the stairs to the office. Seated at Alvera's desk is a new face. A long grayish face framed by mid-length gray hair and punctuated by small, dull brown eyes. Nothing about this face is smiling.

"Hi, I'm Jake, who are you?"

"My name is Donna Tettus, Mr. Brand."

"I see. Are you filling in for Alvera?"

"No, sir, I'm a temp to replace her."

I stop and stare at Donna. I know that the utter confusion reflected on my face is building Donna's respect for my investigative skills. I decide to further enhance my rep with my verbal skills. "Hunh?"

"Alvera quit yesterday. I'm her temporary replacement." Donna smiles at me and then looks down at papers on her desk that apparently need to be neatly stacked immediately.

"Alvera quit, and Sarah hired you?" Nothing impresses a new staff person more than total confusion.

"Correct."

"I see. Could you get Sarah on the phone for me?"

"Of course."

"Are you always this verbose?"

"Ver-who?"

"Uh, never mind."

I sit behind my desk, and my phone rings. I pick up, and Sarah greets me. "How did it go with Witten?"

"Not on the phone. We can talk when we get back together."

"Oh, okay. So...you've met Donna."

"Uh, yeah. What happened?"

"Oh come on, you know the drill, Alvera quit because you were a pain in the ass."

"I was..."

"Yes."

"Now wait, I didn't..."

"Jake, it's done. Just get to know Donna and make her feel at home. She'll be good for us—just give her a chance."

"Feel at home. What is that?"

"You know, make small talk with her. Charm her like you do all women. Oh wait, I guess that isn't working so well right now. No, don't treat her like a woman; I'd hate to see you get rejected. No, treat her like a new client with loads of money. Hey, I got to go. Practice being a Normal Person, Jake."

My little devil and angel finally agree on something. Unfortunately, they agree that Sarah's right about the charm thing. "Oh yeah, watch this," I say to my imaginary friends. I walk back out and smile at Donna.

"Hey, Donna, what's shaking?"

"What do you mean?"

"I mean, what's shaking, what's happening, what's new?"

"Is there something wrong with the way I'm moving?"

"No, no, no, it's just a figure of speech.

"A figure of speech?"

"Sure, just a different way of saying something. Like instead of saying, 'I'm hungry,' maybe I'll say, 'I could eat a horse.'"

"You eat horse?"

"No, I don't eat horse. I just meant...never mind. Where are my messages?"

"They're on your desk along with bills that need to be paid."

"Thanks, Donna."

I walk into my office and start flipping through messages, bills, correspondence, and junk mail. But I can't concentrate; I can't get Ari's face out of my mind. I toss the papers onto the floor so I don't have to be distracted.

My phone rings, and I pick up. "Hello."

"It's Officer Jenkins, Mr. Brand. He's here to see you," Donna tells me.

"Okay, I'll be right out." What is Jenkins doing here? I walk out to reception and see two cops, all in blue. Donna has failed to mention that Officer Jenkins brought backup. Jenkins is just under six feet, in his mid-forties, and sports a black moustache in contrast to his bald pate. His flat gray eyes are unreadable. His buddy is taller and more muscular. He looks at me like he's waiting for an excuse to knock me to the floor and cuff me.

"Officer Jenkins, it's a pleasure to meet you. How may I help you?" We shake hands as he looks me over. He employs a typical cop trick and tries to use silence to make me uncomfortable. I just stare at him as I wait for his shtick to end.

"Mr. Brand, I was hoping I could have a moment of your time. Is there somewhere private we can speak?"

"Sure, in my office. Right this way."

"Wait here," he says to his backup. The backup nods slightly while never taking his eyes off of me.

I point Jenkins to a chair as I move around my pretend-wood desk and sit in my pretend-leather chair. I pull out a cigarette, light it, and place it in an ashtray just up the air current from me. "Smoke?" I offer Jenkins. "Why is he here?" my little devil asks.

"No, thanks. I take it Tigard doesn't have an indoor smoking prohibition?"

"They may, but since I don't inhale, I'm not smoking. I don't think they have a prohibition against open flames or burning material."

Jenkins laughs and seems to relax. "I spoke to Milt; he said you were a total prick. He didn't mention that you were a total prick with a sense of humor."

"Milt always wants to understate everything. That way he won't be embarrassed when I do something truly odd in front of people who know both of us."

"Like lighting a cigarette and not smoking it?"

"Okay, why is he still here?" My little angel asks.

"Well, technically, I am inhaling the fumes—sort of a secondhand smoking technique. But, Officer, I can't imagine that you came here to search for an open flame."

"No, I heard some news today that reminded me of our previous conversation regarding Mr. Weintraub's murder."

"You have some news?" Why is he here?

"Yes, but before we get into my news, I need to ask you a few questions."

"Shoot."

"Interesting choice of words, Mr. Brand. Do you own a .45 caliber weapon?"

"No."

"I didn't think so. Milt says he's never seen you with one. And we don't show any record of your having ever purchased one. Not that we have very complete records on who owns what guns, mind you. Can you account for your whereabouts in the past couple of hours?"

An hour ago, I was examining Ari's third eye. How the hell did he pick that exact time to ask me about? I need to be very careful with my answers. "I was involved in an investigation in Tualatin. Why?"

"Sorry, Mr. Brand. As soon as I'm done, you can ask all of the questions you'd like. Where in Tualatin were you?"

"I'm afraid that's private information, client related. If you have a subpoena, I'll be happy to lay it all out."

"Actually, Mr. Brand, if you aren't forthcoming, you could be an accessory after the fact. Where in Tualatin were you?"

I think really hard about how to respond. He was helpful before, but he's a cop. But if I want info from him, I'll need to share a little. More important, the wrong lie could land me in jail for a long time.

"I was at the home of Ari Witten. But you know that, don't you?"

"Yes, we have a witness who saw a man who fits your description snooping around Mr. Witten's home. Was Mr. Witten there?"

Jenkins's eyes are smiling—he's enjoying this. And I believe he's giving me a "get out of jail free" card. "Sort of. He was dead in his kitchen."

Jenkins stares at me but not in surprise. "Did you kill him?"

"No, he was dead when I got there. I saw the body, quickly went through the house to see if the killer was still there, and left. I wasn't in the house for more than five minutes."

Jenkins nods his head. "Fortunately for you, Mr. Brand, the witness heard a shot fifteen minutes before you arrived. I know you aren't the killer. But not reporting a crime is a violation of your investigator's license. You could lose it." He stops and watches the angst wash across my face. "Fortunately, a concerned citizen made an anonymous tip to 911. I've heard the tape—sounds amazingly similar to you."

"Officer Jenkins, I have an obligation to report the crime as part of my licensing. But there's nothing I'm aware of that says I have to identify myself."

He leans forward and looks at me very closely. "Are you always so clever? Clever can be dangerous."

I shrug. No reason to go to every fight you're invited to.

"Why Witten? How did you come up with his name?"

Damn, I was hoping he wouldn't go there. I have no way of explaining that I was checking on Witten except because of Alberty. That means the codes to get into the city databases. "I discovered the City of Portland has Leafs in their motor pool. I found out that Witten had used one of the Leafs." I wait for Jenkins to dig deeper. If I tell him about the codes, he investigates Phil and finds Brown.

He nods as he looks at me. "Okay, thanks."

I stare back. "Dodged a bullet there," my little angel says. I decide to change the subject. "You said I could ask some questions." He nods. "What is a Portland cop doing working a Tualatin murder?"

He looks down at his hands and back to me. "We had identified Witten as a person of interest. He was on a watch list that was pinged when his name hit the wires." Jenkins looks around my office. I feel relief that for the first time during his visit he isn't staring at me. "I've reconsidered your offer, Mr. Brand. If you don't mind, I'd like that smoke."

I toss him my pack and my lighter. He lights up, and I can see pleasure spread across his face. "Been a while since you inhaled?"

"Yes. My wife is all over me about giving them up. But you know how it goes. Sometimes it's just the right thing to do. You ever notice that the more important a woman becomes in your life, the more control she has? Oh well, she's just trying to extend my life, I suppose." He exhales toward the ceiling and sadly puts the cigarette out. "See, Mr. Brand, even police have rules to follow. There is one more thing I need. How did you get access to the city's motor pool information? And don't forget that I can still file a complaint against you for not identifying yourself when you called 911. Probably won't stand up but would churn your time and money."

I can't hide my frustration at being pushed around. I look down at my desk and shake my head slightly. I look back at Jenkins and smile as I try to compose myself. "I discovered that the City of Portland owns several Nissan Leafs. Since Tony did business with the city and was perhaps struck by a Leaf, I thought there might be a connection. I asked around and discovered that Witten had one the night Tony was killed. I didn't have any proof that it was Witten. And I didn't have proof that the Nissan was one of the city's cars.

But I thought it was worth asking him some questions." I break for a moment, and before he can begin to speak, I say, "And I reported the crime because it was the right thing to do. I did it timely and didn't disturb the scene. If you want to yank my license because I didn't give you my name, then go for it. But don't sit here and pretend that I did anything wrong."

He smiles and nods. "Fair enough Jake, I was being a cop. Maybe I went too far. It's funny you should mention the city motor pool. We had the same thought. We have a forensic team going over the motor pool Leafs as we speak. What do you know about Mr. Witten?"

"Not much—just that he worked for the city and had access to the Leaf."

"I see. We did some background work on him. Turns out he's a made man. He's part of a syndicate from back East. This is the first we've heard of them reaching this far west. They're dangerous, Mr. Brand. They're old-school thugs and new-school gangsters rolled into one big badass syndicate. For your own safety, I suggest that you keep a low profile.

"In addition, I'm obligated to inform you that this is an active police case. If you continue your 'inquiries,' you could be charged with obstruction. That having been said, Milt assures me that you're going to ignore everything I just told you. So, I'm asking that if you run across anything that could help us, you contact me immediately. I promise I'll keep your confidence."

"Of course. My information is your information."

1:00 p.m.
““Dinner and drinks are on me...” Jake

As soon as Jenkins is gone, I call Sarah, using the burner she bought me a few days ago. “Where are you?”

“I’m running errands, and then I’m going to head back over to Sammy’s. Where are you?”

“I’m at the office. Things are happening fast. I went out to Witten’s, and somebody beat me there. He’d been shot. But that’s not the worst of it.”

“What?”

“They killed his dog. I’m a bit pissed about that. Anyway, I called it in to 911 anonymously, and in less than an hour I got a visit from the Portland cop investigating Tony’s death.”

“What’s a Portland cop doing working a Tualatin murder?”

“He tied Witten to the Leaf, and me to the 911 call. Apparently the cops aren’t very far behind us on this thing. But there are two dead guys and an unidentified killer. I need you to make sure Heather is safe—stay with her.”

“I’ll call you as soon as I get to Sammy’s.”

“Okay. Also, just to be safe, make sure your sister gets out of town. I’ll close the office and have Donna disappear.”

“What should I tell Sammy?”

“Nothing yet. I think Sammy’s clean, but there may be a leak in his crew.”

“Do you have a plan? With Witten dead, we don’t have any leads.”

“I’m working on one. Get to Heather...”

Sarah hangs up, hopefully to focus on driving really fast. I walk out to talk to Donna. “Look, Donna, occasionally we have a drill where we all head somewhere private for a few days. Do you have a relative you could stay with for a while? There's extra cash for expenses, and you still get your salary."

"You're paying me to stay away from the office?" she asks as I hustle her toward the door.

"Correct, and your home. If you don't have a relative to stay with, find a nice hotel downtown. Dinner and drinks are on me."

"Mr. Brand, you're scaring me. Should I be afraid?"

"No, Donna, just be safe. Don't talk to strangers; just enjoy yourself for a couple of days. This is just a precaution."

"Oh boy, we're up the creek. I can see it in your creepy smile. Mr. Brand, you don't need to pay me while I'm gone, because I'm not coming back. I don't want to worry about hiding out and being attacked."

"Donna, no one's going to attack you. I assure you you're safe. As soon as this is over, I'll call you, and we can talk about it over coffee."

"Nope, no way, no how. I don't need this sort of thing. I just want a place to work. Goodbye, Mr. Brand, and I do mean goodbye." Donna leaves about as quickly as anyone has from this office.

I move back to my office and try to think of what to do next. "Fire up the bourbon, dude," my little devil says. Right, bourbon, get drunk—that will keep Heather and Sarah alive. I lock my little devil in a closet and work on constructive thoughts. Right now I need to know that Heather is safe at Sammy's. My phone rings; it's Sarah.

"Well?"

"She's not at Sammy's. She told someone on his staff she

had a couple of items to pick up at home. I called her house and on the burner we gave her, but she didn't pick up on either of them. I'm on my way over there now."

"Call me as soon as you get there." We hang up, and I start reviewing the pieces. Tony's dead, hit by a car. His executioner is dead, shot point-blank. And now Heather is missing. The only lead I have is Tony's partner, Phil. I decide I need to poke him with a stick.

2:00 p.m.
"Two dead bodies..." Jenkins

When I'm on my way to Phil's, Sarah calls to let me know Heather isn't at her home. I ask Sarah to meet me at Phil's building so we can pound on the bastard. For most of the drive, I harangue myself for not controlling Heather better. How in the world could I let her slip through my fingers?

Sarah and I meet in the building lobby and ride the elevator up to Phil's floor. The elevator door opens and frames a burly cop standing with his hands on his hips and a bored look on his face.

"I'm sorry—this is a restricted area," he tells us.

"Excuse me, Officer, what's happening?"

"I'm not at liberty to discuss. You'll need to go back down the elevator—this is a crime scene."

"Let them through, Craig."

I look over Craig's shoulder and see Officer Jenkins walking toward us.

"Mr. Brand, why am I not surprised you're here? Don't answer just yet. Who are you?" he asks Sarah.

"This is Sarah Genton. She's my assistant. Sarah, this is Officer Al Jenkins."

"Come with me, please, both of you." He leads us into an empty office, closes the door, pulls up a chair, and waits as we sit. "Mr. Brand, this is the second crime scene you've been to today. What gives?"

"Al—"

"Jenkins, Officer Jenkins."

"Oh, of course, Officer Jenkins. I don't know anything. We were just on our way to meet with Phil—"

"Who's dead."

"Phil's dead?" I feel despair running after me. Phil was my next to last lead. My only other lead, more a prayer, is to confront Sammy and accuse his staff. But I don't have a name, any evidence, only a couple of coincidences.

"Cut the bullshit. This is two dead bodies in just a few hours. I told you that if you meddled in an investigation I would arrest and charge you. Even if the charges don't stick, you'll be out of the way in a jail cell. I'm done playing good cop. What the hell do you know? Was Mr. Alberty involved in Mr. Weintraub's death?"

"I don't know."

"But you were coming to see him almost immediately after hearing of Mr. Witten's death."

"Well, not almost immediately. I read mail, sorted emails, let my secretary go..."

"Donna's gone?" Sarah asks.

"Yeah, she wasn't happy boxed up in the office all by herself."

"Damn it, Jake, you chased another one away. How many is that this year?"

"Stop it," Jenkins says. "Focus on me. I'm the one with handcuffs and the authority to imprison you for the rest of your goddamn lives."

"She really wasn't that good," I whisper to Sarah.

"How the hell would you know? You only knew her for twelve seconds."

"Stop! Both of you stop bickering." Jenkins looks at us like he's trying to stop two three-year-olds from fighting over a Stretch Armstrong doll. "Last chance, Mr. Brand. What do you know?"

I take my time to measure my words. I have to share enough to stay out of jail but not enough that I end up on Sammy's bad side. "I already told you that I think Witten killed Tony using a city motor pool car. But I don't have proof. I spoke to Phil the other day, and he had suspicions that someone at the city could have been involved. When I learned that Witten was dead, my only lead was Phil. So, we came to talk to Phil. Obviously, somebody beat me to him."

"Obviously. Why do you think he could have known about Witten?"

"Tony had told Phil that he thought he was being followed by someone from the city. Witten worked for the city. Phil told me he had access to the city databases. Phil could have checked out the Leaf on his own."

Jenkins looks at me for a moment. "You didn't mention the database when we met earlier."

"I didn't think it had anything to do with Witten's death."

"You don't get to make those choices. I decide what's important and what isn't. What else aren't you telling me, Brand?"

"That you're a snarly jerk," says my little devil.

"Nothing. I don't think there's anything else I could share."

Jenkins stares at me. I can feel his innate lie detector measuring my relative level of truthfulness. I'm afraid that he's going to start going through Alberty's Rolodex and somehow tie all of this to Sammy. If he does that, he might trip over Phil and Tony's connection to Sammy. "So, somebody killed Phil in his office?"

"No, he was killed in the parking garage. The coroner says he was strangled. Mr. Brand, I wish I could hold you, because I know you're holding out on me. But I can't prove it, at least not yet. You two should leave before you say the wrong thing."

"Officer Jenkins—" Sarah begins.

Jenkins turns toward Sarah, smiles, and says, "Call me Al."

"Al, if we hear anything, we'll be sure to give you a call."

"I'm sure you will, Sarah. As for Jake? Well, just look at his track record so far."

3:00 p.m.
"No one's tried to contact us..." Sarah

We leave the building and find a coffee shop so we can strategize. Sarah tries calling Heather on her burner and even tries her home line, with no luck. She asks, "What now?"

"I'll head over to her house. Earlier when you checked on her, did you go inside?"

"Yes, I had to break a window in the back, but I went through the place and didn't see anything."

"Okay, I'll take a second look. I'll give Sammy a call. You go back to the office and check phone messages. Forward the phones to your cell and go someplace safe. Oh, and turn your regular phone on. We need to be reachable but not traceable. Either Heather's getting a spa treatment or someone has her. She has no value without the drive, so their next move is to contact us."

I feel Sarah examining me for cracks.

I look at her and smile; I'm sure it's not a radiant smile, but it's the best I can project at the moment. "I'm fine. And she's fine as well. Somebody will contact us soon."

We head off in our different directions. From the car I call Sammy's number. Someone answers and hands Sammy the phone.

"Jake, have you found Heather?"

"No, I was hoping you had."

"No, nothing.

"Sammy, I need to update you on a couple of things." I tell him about Witten and Alberty. I don't give him any details, just the broad strokes.

"You say the cop is Jenkins?" Sammy asks.

"Yeah, Al Jenkins. He's connected Witten, Tony, and Phil. He's got to be going through Phil's rolodex."

"I'll check him out. You take care of finding Heather—I'll figure out the rest. I got to go, Jake; keep me updated."

"I will. The number I'm calling from is my contact number. Give me a call if you hear anything.

"Absolutely. Oh, and I'll check with my boys and see if maybe we can come up with a lead."

"Thanks, Sammy." I hang up and focus on driving. Just to be thorough, and since it's on my way, I stop at Franklin's tavern and pull him aside for a chat. He swears he hasn't heard anything from Heather. He seems genuinely concerned and promises to contact me if he does. He offers me a drink, and I hesitate. One drink can't be all that bad. "One means two," my little angel says. I tell Franklin no, thanks.

I arrive at Heather's home, a one-story contemporary with a washed-brick facade. Just as Sarah told me, everything is locked up. Out back, I find the broken window and enter the house. All of the lights are off, but there's still enough natural light that I can find my way around without turning lights on. I move through a kitchen into a living room. Then I move down a hallway, past a bathroom and a bedroom. So far, everything looks normal. At the end of the hall is one more bedroom. I look around but don't see any signs of a struggle or a clue that's going to help us find Heather. I see a picture of Tony and Heather on a nightstand. I pick it up. They look happy. As hard as I try, I can't help but imagine me in that picture instead of Tony. All those years of memories of her—what if they had been experiences with her instead? Now he's dead, and she's missing. I call Sarah. "Have you found anything?"

"No, I'm at the office, and no one's tried to contact us. Did you find anything?"

"No, nothing."

"What now?"

What now? "Hey, we should beat the snot out of somebody—that always feels good," my little devil says.

"Jake, are you there?"

"I'm here. Right now continue to monitor email and the phones and stay somewhere safe. Don't go home, go to a hotel. Go to a nice hotel. Let's contact each other every thirty minutes so we know we're okay."

"Okay, what are you going to do?"

Good question. What is tough-guy Brand going to do? "I'm going to hang out here for a while until I think of a better place to be. I'll call Milt and see if he has any suggestions other than rolling out the cops."

"Jake, I know you want to protect Sammy, but maybe you should have the police take a look at him."

"I will, if Milt doesn't have other ideas. But it doesn't do us any good to save Heather from bad guys, assuming they have her, only to be on Sammy's hit list. No, in a few hours, maybe."

"Got it. I'm sure she's fine."

"I agree. Be careful, Sarah."

We hang up, and I call Milt. I go through what I have, and the only idea he has is to put out a missing person report. He agrees to do it using Heather's maiden name rather than her married name. I hope that we'll keep her from popping up on Jenkins's watch list. The last thing I need is Jenkins asking about Heather's connection to all of this. I find my way back to the kitchen and open the fridge. I reach past the white wine, grab a Diet Coke, and sit at the table and sip. Someone had to have grabbed her; it's the only explanation that fits. But who and why? The most obvious why is the flash drive, but now that Ari's dead and Sammy has the drive, I don't have another lead. But what if it isn't the drive—what if there's something else going on? I struggle back and forth with my thoughts and check in with Sarah every thirty minutes. But most of the time I worry about Heather. What if she's hurt, or worse? If someone has hurt her, I will find them.

8:00 p.m.
"You can't just storm in..." Sarah

I'm no closer to a solution when my phone buzzes. It's telling me I have a text message from an unknown caller. I press a few buttons and see a picture of Heather. She's seated, gagged, and bound. Beneath her picture is an address on the east side of town and an invitation to be there, alone, no later than nine tonight.

My emotions are mixed. I'm happy because she's alive, but I'm fearful because she's in danger. I touch the picture of her face with my finger. I forward the text to Sarah and call her.

"Did you get the text?"

"Jake, she's alive. That's good news. What do we do now?"

"I go get her."

"You can't just storm in. Do you know anything about that location?" Sarah asks.

"I'm guessing it's a warehouse. Right neighborhood and right kind of building to hide out in."

"Maybe it's time to call Milt again," Sarah says.

"Not yet—he won't be able to downplay this one. And if

we involve the police, we're back to being on Sammy's dark side. No, I think we should call Sammy."

"Sammy? How the hell do you know Sammy didn't send the picture?"

"Why would he? We gave him our word we wouldn't say anything. He knows that we know the consequences of not keeping our commitment. Plus, if he wanted me, he'd just show up at my door. No, this isn't Sammy. I think Sammy is on our side with this. "

"Who do you think has her?"

"I haven't the foggiest. Our only hope is to go to the location and meet him or her. But you and I aren't enough muscle. We need backup, and Sammy is all we have access to. Plus, Sammy needs Phil's killer caught quickly, or the police are going to go through Phil's files. There's a good chance they'll stumble onto Brown Construction. No, I think Sammy will want this guy as badly as we do. And Sarah, I need you to stay out of the way. I don't want to be saving you as well as Heather."

"You can be such a bastard. I can take care of myself. I'm going to be there for Heather and for you whether you like it or not."

I smile. "Thanks, Sarah." I dial Sammy's number.

"I assume that you've heard something." says Sammy.

"Yes, and I need your help. I received a text message saying Heather's being held and they want me."

I hear silence as the wheels turn in Lake Oswego.

"Sammy, I can't do this alone."

"Where should we meet you, Jake?"

9:00 p.m.
"My finger could twitch..." Bad Guy

The east side warehouse district runs along the Willamette River opposite downtown Portland. It has some of the prettiest views of the city. Right along the edge of the district and directly between it and the river are tangled lanes of freeway. The address that I received is two blocks up from the river. The building is a two-story beige structure that encompasses an entire block. I circle the building but don't see any indication of inhabitants. The exterior is nondescript, with no company signage.

I'm anxious at entering on their terms. I hope the bad guys will feel relaxed and take their time before they dismember me or force me to watch old episodes of *Matlock*. It's uncomfortable to have to depend on others, but I'll need my backup to turn the tables and give me some playing power. I park and watch what appears to be the main entrance for a few minutes. I find it difficult to move toward the door. But it's inevitable. I exit my car, walk to the door, pull out my .38, and find the door unlocked. I step across the threshold into the yawning darkness. As I do, I pull a small roll of duct tape from my pocket and place a piece across the latch. I'm not sure Mr. Duct anticipated this function when he was in his lab. The tape will prevent someone from locking the door behind me.

I stand perfectly still as my eyes adjust to the darkness. A small amount of light filters in through windows placed high on the wall and mixes with the glow of a few red exit signs. Massive metal racks holding boxes stand forty feet high, nearly to the ceiling.

I hear movement to my right and turn toward a shadow that slowly transforms into a man holding a shotgun aimed at my foam-insulated six-pack.

"Set your gun on the ground and kick to me. And don't leave it short—my finger could twitch if I have to move toward you to pick it up."

I set my gun on the ground and give it a kick so it slides past him. I hope he can't see my smile in the dark. "Whoops."

"You're ballsy, gotta give you that. Move away from the door."

He retrieves my gun and then moves to the door. I've decided that my best strategy is to keep him talking and get him frustrated. Frustrated people thinking about seemingly meaningless tasks make mistakes.

"I have to say, you aren't very hospitable. I'm not sure I'm going to invite you over to my place to play canasta."

"Shut the fuck up." He pulls a key out of his pocket and uses it to lock the door. Just as he's about to check the door handle to make sure the door is secure, I move to the side, out of his range of vision. He twists to keep me in sight and forgets to confirm the door is locked.

"Whoa nelly, why are you so nervous? I'm unarmed, I'm an invited guest, and you haven't even introduced yourself. My name is Jake—what's yours?"

"You can call me Twelve Gauge."

"I'm not sure I like that so much. How about I call you Twelve, like, preteen?"

"You have a death wish? What don't you understand about which end of the gun is pointed at you? Shut up and move straight ahead. You'll see a light once you get around the first rack. Move straight to the light. Any sideways move could get you killed."

"Ahh, move toward the light. I get it. This way?" I point to what I think is the wrong direction.

"No, to the right. Stop wasting time."

"Okay, okay, I just don't want us to get lost in here. Do you work here? It looks kind of complex."

"Move, and for the third time, shut...the fuck...up."

"I'm just trying to—"

The ass hits me square in the back with the butt of the gun and knocks me to my knees. "Are you starting to get the picture? If not, I can do some more paintin'."

I can see his shoes two feet away. He's feeling good about himself, strong and powerful. I stand and look him in the eye. He's about six feet six inches, two fifty. In the limited light I can't tell his eye color, but I can see that his head is shaved. I don't recognize him.

"Move."

I smile, turn, and walk. I walk slowly. I observe how the racks are laid out and where there are doors and windows. There's a slight chemical smell interwoven with dust. We move about halfway through the building and enter a lit, open space. In the middle is a desk and chair. Sitting on the chair is Heather. Her hands are secured behind her, and she's gagged. Her eyes are red and scared; her hair's a tangled mess. How is it possible that she can be so beautiful, even in such desperate circumstances? I'm feeling like this guy has earned a little bit of angry Jake. Assuming I can disarm them.

"Hey, babe, you okay?"

She nods and then nervously looks to my right.

"Jake Brand, what a pleasant surprise. I take it you've come to save your damsel?"

Without turning, I recognize the voice. It's Sammy's second-favorite nephew, Benny.

"Look who's got big-boy pants. Benny...I don't think I ever heard your last name, by the way."

"Don't matter, at least it don't to you. Tracy here said you'd bring cops. I said no way. Brand is all testosterone, a real tough guy. Remember when we met? When you put a gun to my head?" Benny moves up to me and presses a gun to my forehead. He's feeling good about the current arrangement.

"I do remember, Benny. I remember how sweaty your hands were. You must have been scared shitless."

"You don't seem to understand the situation. I'm going to kill you. If you cooperate, maybe I let the bitch live. For a while anyway." He smiles at me.

"*Maybe* you'll kill me. But right now I think you need something. Otherwise I'd already be dead, wouldn't I?"

"Very good, Brand. There is something you could do for me."

"What's that?"

"Well, I need some help on a business transaction. I need a competitor put out of business, so to speak."

"Ahh, is it safe to say that this competitor is related to you?"

"Very safe. The way I figure, you take care of my problem, I let you and the girl live a little bit longer. What do you say?"

"Umm, no, I don't think so. How about I offer a third option? You and Tracy put your guns down, and I take you in to the cops. You confess to murdering Phil and Ari and setting up Tony. Then maybe Sammy lets you live in prison."

"I had nothing to do with Phil. You ain't so smart after all, are you? Plus, you know Sammy ain't going to let me live. No way, no how; I've crossed his line. What a bunch of bullshit, him and his line. The line is exactly where he wants it to be when he wants it to be there. I'm tired of slaving for that prick. No, I like my idea better. Get on your knees."

"I don't think so."

Benny walks over to Heather and puts the gun to her temple. She twists and turns against the bindings, which makes Benny snicker. "Pretty please?"

Slowly I lower to my knees, facing Heather. Fear is gripping her. I discretely wink at her. I try to reduce her anxiety by projecting confidence. Benny walks over to me and places the gun to my head. I work hard at not showing my anxiety. There's nothing in this world quite as sobering as the metal barrel of a gun pressed against your head, with the finger of a thug on its trigger.

"Last chance, pretty boy. Are you working for me or you working for the worms?"

"You drive a hard bargain, Benny. Will I need an attorney to review contracts? Or is this one of those 'my word is my bond' deals?"

"Tracy, cut one of her fingers off."

Heather squirms and emits a muffled scream.

"You're right, no attorneys. Let her go, and we've got a deal."

"No way. She's my leverage. Until you complete your assignment, she stays with me. Oh, and she'll be paying the interest on your debt if you ain't quick about it. Know what I mean?"

Before I can respond, I sense movement from multiple directions. I sense Benny jerking his head around while still pointing his gun at my head. I hear a whisper from behind me.

"Benny, put the gun down."

"Sammy, no way. I—"

"Shhh, there's no need to talk, Benny. I understand your thinking. I remember when my old man was aging. Before he went to prison, I thought I was smarter and stronger than him. I squared off against him once and learned a valuable lesson. He beat the stuffing out of me." Sammy is walking toward Benny as he talks. There are five other armed men with weapons pointed at Benny and Tracy. Sarah is with them, her weapon drawn, too.

"I was laid up for two weeks. When I was back on my feet, my pop told me, 'Sammy, it's okay to want more. Just make sure you can carry the weight.' You know what he meant, Benny?"

Benny shakes his head. In the dim light I can see perspiration on his forehead. His eyes desperately search for an escape. Sammy stops in front of Benny. Their noses are separated by a hair. Sammy doesn't blink and doesn't stop glaring directly into Benny's eyes. Benny is mesmerized, as if Sammy were a cobra poised to strike. He begins to shake and tries to say something, but only manages a stutter. Even though Benny is at least four inches taller than his uncle, Sammy towers over him.

Sammy leans in to Benny's ear and whispers, "Give me the gun, Benny." And he does.

Wednesday, July 27

9:00 a.m.
"Recently lost two fingers..." Jenkins

Last night, after Sammy took control at the warehouse, he politely asked Sarah, Heather, and me to leave. He wanted to have a family meeting. As we left the warehouse, Heather broke into uncontrollable sobs. Her emotional release echoed between the empty buildings and touched me deeply. Sarah and I both comforted her, and I invited them both to spend the night at my condo. We put Heather into my bed after a couple shots of good scotch. I lay on the couch, pretending to sleep for about an hour and then wandered over to my bedroom. I opened the door and hesitated, unsure of what my next move was until I heard Heather.

"How long are you going to stand there staring at me?"

"I haven't decided." I waited a beat. "I think that's been long enough. How about you?"

"It's been too long. Get your butt over here, Jake Brand."

I tried not to run and jump. I tried to be as suave and debonair as I could. But I don't think how I got there mattered. As soon as I was between the sheets, Heather grabbed me like I was a life ring and she was drowning. We kissed for a few minutes, and then she cuddled to my chest and fell asleep. Her nearness distracted my attempts at slumbering, despite my exhausted state. Her softness and warmth were exhilarating. Once I fell asleep, we slept like an old married couple. It felt comfortable to me, especially this morning, when I watched her wake, see me, and smile.

Now, I get up and head to the kitchen to start making breakfast. Sarah is up and looks at me sadly as I come out of my room. I know she thinks Heather is wrong for me, but something inside says it's more complex than that.

Heather and I make breakfast together. I clean the dishes while she showers. She washes my back while I shower. But as much as I want to continue playing house, I need to head to the office and keep those pesky clients happy.

After several days of chasing and being chased, I struggle to slow my mind to an everyday pace; having Heather near was helping. At the office, I just can't get started. I try to read my emails, but I still feel that gun pressed against my head. I try to return calls, but I see Heather tied to a chair. I also feel Heather in my arms sleeping peacefully. Is this happiness? Sue and I spent so much time on the edges of our bed that I hardly remember us holding each other.

After near-death experiences, I find I crawl into myself. I revisit the experience and grade my performance. I feel pretty good about this one, at least the dangerous parts. But I've still got thoughts to occupy my mind. I'm conflicted about reuniting with Heather. I think about the image of Heather I've carried with me for years. And I think about the Heather of the past few days. I think about the possibility of being with the Heather, of being a couple. And I'm anxious about the risk of being hurt again. Plus, I'm still sorting through my divorce from Sue. I sense Sue on the periphery of my thoughts, but falling further and further into the past. I hear the door to the office open and close. I hold my .38 under my desk and wait for company to arrive. Yeah, maybe I'm still a bit jumpy.

"Brand, are you here? I was told you were here."

I recognize Jenkins's voice. I put my gun in a drawer, light up a cigarette, and invite him back as I place it in an ashtray.

"Good morning, Officer. What brings you out to Tigard, this early a.m.?"

"Oh, I think you know." He says it with no expression on his face. He waits for me to give away what I know.

"Oh, I don't think I do." I stare at him, clearly indicating that I'm done talking until he says something interesting.

He looks back at me with an "I'm about to catch you in a lie" look. I stare right back with an "I'm a better liar than you think" look. "This morning Benjamin Manti and Tracy Free entered a precinct house and confessed to the murders of Anthony Weintraub, Phillip Alberty, and Ari Witten. It seems that Manti and Free were securing sweetheart construction deals from the city using Alberty and Witten as go-betweens. Manti and Free discovered that Alberty was skimming, so they took everybody out."

He pauses and looks at me for a response. I say and do nothing. I know the confession is false, if only because Ari killed Tony.

"But I have two questions that I thought you might be able to clear up."

"Shoot."

"First, Manti had recently lost two fingers. Free was missing a few teeth. They say they lost them in a card game. You wouldn't happen to know of any card games that allow body parts as a wager, would you?"

"Nope."

Jenkins stares at me, waiting for me to expand on my in-depth analysis.

"I see."

"And number two?" I ask.

"Yes, number two. There's a warehouse on the east side that happens to have security cameras. Last night all but one was turned off. The one operating camera was pointed toward a door. The video is pretty grainy, but we got some info off of it. At approximately 9:00 p.m. the door opened and an individual entered. This individual looks a lot like you. After a few seconds, a second individual enters the shot. The second individual can be identified as Tracy Free. I wonder, if we could zoom in close enough and clean up the image like they do on TV if we'd see that at this point his teeth were still his to lose." Jenkins stops again and tries to read my eyes. "Sure you don't know anything about Manti and Free and what happened last night?"

"I'm sure."

"You have another smoke?"

"Of course. Anything for an officer sworn to serve and protect." I toss him my pack and my lighter.

He lights up and blows smoke rings at the ceiling. "Just so we're clear, on another day, in different circumstances, you'd be cuffed and behind bars. You know that, right?"

I smile.

He smiles back and stands. "Good day, Jake. If you ever need help in the future, don't hesitate to call someone else."

"That's very kind of you, Al."

10:00 a.m.
"You know I'm armed, right?" Jake

An hour after Jenkins leaves, Sarah comes in.

"I thought you were going to keep Heather company?"

"She seemed fine and told me to go ahead and leave. She was headed home to try to start her life again."

"I see."

"That's not all she said."

"Oh?"

"Yeah."

I watch Sarah and wait expectantly for a punch line that seems trapped in her head. "Are you going to tell me what else she said?"

She looks at me and seems to be measuring her words. "I haven't decided."

"You've decided to tell me she said something, but you're undecided on whether or not you're going to tell me what it is that she said?"

"Yeah."

My little devil says, "Ahhhhh my God, she's so mean."

"You know I'm armed, right?" I ask.

"You're going to have to do better than that if you want to know what I know."

"Tell me, or I'll ask Heather to move in with me. You could move in too; we can be a modern-day *Three's Company*."

"Oooo, you win. She asked me to let you know she'd be at her house if you *needed* her for *anything*." She emphasized the words just like that. "Oh, I can't believe I said that. It's almost as bad as throwing up. I need to go brush my teeth."

Sarah moves to leave my office but stops and turns back. "She'll break you, Jake." A brief melancholy smile and she disappears.

I sit back in my chair to think. She'll break me? I'm already broken, haunted by a dream of a young woman, hurt by the dismantling of my marriage, fighting my own bad choices. Is it possible to be any more broken? "You are such...a whiner! Grow up," my little angel says. "I didn't think it was possible, but I agree with Batboy. What about Carl, and Milt, your family...what about Sarah?" my little devil asks.

Crap, can't I have five minutes to myself?

12:01 p.m.
"You just need to let loose..." Heather

I stand on Heather's porch, hesitating to knock. I feel like a kid. I feel like I'm standing in the moonlight, looking at a window, hoping it's open and wondering what awaits me on the other side. The excitement of the unknown and of the possible rage through my brain. I want with every fiber of my being to be that kid again. I want to believe that last night was a real beginning. But as always, the stark darkness of the following Monday at school slams into me. I feel my anger from Tony's glibness and my pain from Heather's confession in a deep recess of my heart.

I knock and hear her call to come in. I find her sitting on the couch with photo albums scattered around. She's been crying.

"Sit by me, Jake."

I move to her side on the couch.

"Thanks for saving my life. And don't say it was nothing; I, at least, put more value on my life than nothing."

"I would never say that."

"Oh, what were you going to say?"

"Ahh, it weren't no big deal."

She laughs and shakes her head. "You were always funny, Jake. You'd be funny, and then you'd be quiet. You always thought about things more than Tony and I did. I used to think it meant you were mad. But it didn't, did it? It just meant you needed time to process."

"Most of the time I needed to process, but not always. Sometimes I was mad; sometimes I was angry and wanted to hit someone or something. I learned later in life how to vent that emotion. I still struggle to contain myself at times."

"Maybe that's not the right thing to do. Maybe you just need to let loose and live out your emotions?"

"I tried that and spent a bunch of years in the army. No, I think I'm a containment kind of guy."

"I see that. Jake, I want you to know how special you are to me. I've always loved you. I love you more today than I ever have. I've always considered you my best friend. You were always a better friend to me than Tony was, even when we were married. I think in some ways that made it easier to be with Tony. I wanted both of you around me, and I thought the only way to do that was for you to be a friend first."

"I love you too, and I've never forgotten how close we were."

"How well do you remember that night?" Heather looks at me with hopeful eyes.

"Vividly. I remember your nightgown had a blue ribbon tied in a bow across your chest. I remember your hair was longer than it is now and that your eyes were clear blue orbs that could see to my soul."

"I remember your strength. You were the strongest boy I'd ever met. You were high energy that night. I felt you could protect me from anything. I remember your smell; it was such a boy smell, and I loved it. I wished I could bottle it and keep it with me. I remember your nervousness and how I had to relax you. I remember it as one of the happiest moments of my life. I also remember how hurt you were when you found out about Tony and me.

"Jake, I can't promise forever. But I'd like to try for the now. I'd like to be us for a while."

She smiles at me and softly kisses my lips. I close my eyes and see the young girl and the Heather of today. I drift with the emotional and physical connection. I place my hand on the back of her neck; I feel her soft hair and smell her perfume. "I want that too, Heather."

We move to her bedroom.

Friday, August 5

7:00 p.m.
"Who brings a gun to a card game?" Jake

A week later I drive to Sammy's home on the lake. I've been trying to contact him to warn him that Jenkins has a tape. Even though Jenkins didn't mention Sammy, he has to have seen Sammy and his band of merry men come through the door. Plus, there's a couple of other things that have been bothering me, and I want to clear them up with Sammy.

I couldn't get a hold of Sammy—not by phone, not by messenger, not in person; he was always busy. But I was invited to a big-boy poker game at his place. I drive up to the front of his house, where valets are positioned. I look around and don't see any cars that cost less than a hundred grand or that are more than two years old. I watch as the valets fight over who's stuck with parking my wise old Jeep. I stop in front, and the loser reluctantly comes to get my keys. I hand him a twenty and his eyes light up. "Be careful—I don't want any dings."

"No, sir, though I'm not sure how you'd be able to tell. She's got a few already."

"And I know every one of them. Take that guy right there. That's where I ran a bicyclist off the road. And that one over there? That happened when I pushed a thug into a guardrail. I'd hate to be telling the next valet about the new valet scar." I look at him with just a wee bit of intensity. He looks at the car nervously and then back at me.

"Yeah, right," he says, not entirely sure if I'm as crazy as I seem.

I walk up the front steps, and two guards step in front of me. They confirm that I've been invited and begin to check me with a handheld metal detector.

"Whoa, guys, who brings a gun to a card game?"

"You'd be surprised. But actually, guns are okay. This is looking for recording devices. I'll need your phone. You can pick it up when you leave." I hand him my phone, and he hands me a receipt.

"Okay, I have to ask: am I the only unarmed guest?"

"No, but you're in the minority."

"Perfect. I guess I better lose."

"Have a nice evening, sir."

I enter and am directed to a large room set with ten tables of ten. Well-dressed men and women are socializing and drinking. They all look like they're used to winning and being waited on. I walk to the bar and order a Manhattan up. I finish my first sip, the first sip of alcohol in several days, when a hand is placed on my shoulder. I turn to see Sammy.

"Hey, Sammy, thanks for the invite. I love poker, and you'll love me because I'm terrible at it."

"Oh, Jake, don't say that. I'm comping you the entry fee. If you win, you pay me back. Where's Heather? I hear the two of you have become quite the thing?"

"She's out shopping with a friend. She said something about stinky cigars and men not being her thing. That's very generous of you to comp me. But before the game gets moving, I need to talk to you. It's important."

"Sure, let's go to my study."

As we walk through the crowd, I recognize politicians and local celebrities. There are even a couple of Trail Blazer basketball players in attendance. I feel like a kernel of corn in a tin full of caviar. Once inside Sammy's den, I close the door behind us.

"What's up, Jake?"

"Three things. First, I've been thinking that Benny couldn't have been acting on his own. There had to be someone who was working him. Plus, I was told Witten was connected to another organization."

"Why would you worry about that?"

"They could still use Heather or me as leverage. I'd like to know this is over."

He smiles at me. "It's over. I contacted some friends back East. Arrangements have been made. What else?"

"Second, I wanted to warn you. There's a cop who has a videotape from the warehouse from the night with Benny. Apparently Benny was too stupid to turn all of the cameras off. The cop questioned me, but he must have seen you as well."

Sammy smiles and walks to his desk. He retrieves two cigars from a humidor and hands me one along with a clipper and matches. "I'm told that the proper way to light a cigar is to warm the end for a few seconds before you actually light it. Try it."

Sammy doesn't seem to care about the tape. If anything, he's amused. Not exactly what I expected; freaked out or angry, but not amused. I begin the process of lighting my cigar. "And the video?"

"Jake, remember when I said Benny was my second-favorite nephew?"

"Sure."

“Well, my favorite nephew is my wife’s brother’s son, Alphonse Jenkins. He’s been a very caring nephew. I hold him in high regard.” He pauses and smiles at me while it sinks in.

“There never was a video—it was a test,” my little angel says. “Holy shit,” my little devil says.

“Al wanted to be sure about you. He’s very protective. After I told him that Benny had told you that he didn’t do Phil, Al thought you might publicly question Benny’s confession. We weren’t comfortable with that. Al thought he’d give you a chance to choose your fate.” Sammy leans toward me and whispers, “From where I sit, Jakester, you are a man of your word.” After a brief pause, Sammy asks, “What was the other thing?”

“The other thing? Oh, nothing.” The other thing was Phil; but Sammy beat me to the punch line.

Sunday, September 25

7:40 a.m.
"Traded booze and tobacco for steroids..." Carl

The misty rain coats me like a cold sweat. Running in Portland with any commitment requires love of rain. Or at least acceptance of getting wet. Many people see rain clouds as a dreary dark grayness that shrouds the otherwise green city. But true Oregonians know that rain is a sanctuary. Rain creates a sense of aloneness, interrupted by the blurred trunk of a tall fir and sword ferns. Running in the rain helps me to clear my mind.

Carl is at my shoulder, keeping pace. He's been the best of friends, helping me through my rough spot. Shortly after the madness surrounding Tony's death ended, he challenged me to run with him most days at 6:00 a.m. We've been meeting at different locations and working up distances. At first, I couldn't keep up with him past a couple of miles. Now, once a week we go thirteen miles along a mostly wooded trail in the hills west of downtown.

Today is our long run, and we have one mile to go. I feel strong. I feel as good now as I did when we started. I sense weakness in Carl. I increase my pace slightly. I don't look at Carl as he slips a step behind, but I sense his inner warrior saying, "No way." He increases his pace to get back to my shoulder.

I still lament the failure of my marriage, but it doesn't hurt too much. It will probably end up being a good thing.

With three-quarters of a mile to go, I increase my pace again. Again Carl slips behind a step. Only this time he hangs there, increasing his pace to match mine but not enough to catch up the lost step.

Heather and I have been hot and heavy, spending large chunks of time together. I feel like I'm getting to know her better than I did when we were kids. And I like what I've learned. I enjoy her company, her wit, and her craziness. I never thought of myself as reserved, but compared to Heather, I'm an eighty-year-old man when it comes to spontaneity.

With half a mile remaining, I increase yet again. Now I can feel Carl losing a stride for every few that I take. Sarah has been great. She's helped manage the practice and kept a watchful eye on my bad habits. But mostly she's been a shoulder to lean on when I feel down.

At two hundred yards I sprint. I run with everything I have left. I run from Carl and the past. I finish, slow, and stop. I place my hands behind my head and breathe as much oxygen as I can, through my nose to relieve an ache in my lungs.

"You bastard," says Carl. He's beside me, gasping for air, bent at the waist, with his hands on his knees. "You must have traded booze and tobacco for steroids. You've never been able to beat me, even in the army."

"No steroids, my friend, just clean living." I look at Carl and see my friends who stood by me when I was down. "Carl, if I haven't said it already, thanks. Thanks for confronting me. Thanks for this."

He smiles, and claps me on the back. "I know you'd do the same for me, Jake. That's where friendships are most important."

Thursday, October 27

10:40 p.m.
"A sentry marking the man's territory..." Jake

Winter is here in full force. The trees have shed most of their leaves, and they lie on the ground, slowly turning to mush in the constant rain. Twisted tree branches stand out in the glow of the streetlight, exposed and seemingly lifeless. A biting wind moves the bushes and tree branches in a gentle swaying dance. I glance over at the house. Its lights give me the feeling of warmth. But it's just in my mind. Sitting in my Jeep, with a cigarette in the ash tray and my window open, I feel the briskness in the air. The cold keeps me alert. I wouldn't want a neighbor to sneak up on me, snap a picture with his smartphone, and post it on the internet with a label of *neighborhood perv*.

Heather is amazing. The past several months have been what I always dreamed they could be. We spend most weekends together and usually a few nights during the week. I've started thinking about the next step, the possibility of moving in together. I asked her about that a week ago, and she seemed excited, but didn't have an immediate answer. I shift my sitting position and hear the crinkle of the paper bag. I look down at it and think about the scotch inside. I've controlled my drinking pretty well. I haven't had more than a couple of drinks in an evening in months. But tonight feels special.

The black Volvo sedan sits in the driveway, a sentry marking the man's territory. He's been in the house for at least two hours, as long as I've been parked in my current location. The lovers are foolish; they haven't made much of an attempt to hide their tryst. Parking in the driveway of her house is a sign of their arrogance. No, not arrogance—honesty. Yeah, they are honest about their passion. They don't want to hide; they don't think there's any harm in what they do. They don't care about their significant others. They just care about their moment together: no tomorrows, no yesterdays, just now.

I pull the bottle from the bag and read the label. I'm not looking for information; I'm delaying the act of twisting the foil off of the cap. That's the most important decision. Do I tear the foil off? If I do, I doubt very much that I won't remove the cap, move the narrow glass neck to my lips, and tip my head back. I can anticipate the fluid heating me from the inside out and giving power to my feelings of despair. That foil is all that stands between me and the bottom of the bottle. I know that all of the things I've worked on over the past few months, cutting back on drinking and smoking and increasing exercise, will speed past like a signpost in my rearview mirror.

I look over at her house and imagine them inside, laughing over a funny anecdote. Or maybe they're sitting by a fire in the living room, sharing a bottle of wine and soft kisses. I look back at the bottle and the amber poison it contains. Slowly, I put the bottle back into the paper bag and set it on the passenger side floor of the Jeep. I close my eyes and I see Heather as a teen in a cotton nightgown, lit by the moonlight.

I look back at Heather's house just as the inside lights go out, with him still inside. I turn the key, start the engine, and drive home.